# THE SUPER

TIER



ISBN 979-8-9932675-3-1 (eBook)

ISBN 979-8-9932675-4-8 (Print)

First edition 2026

Visit the author's website at *www.dlmaddox.com*.

Published by TIER Books LLC

A CONSPIRACY THRILLER

# THE SUPER

BOOK 1 IN THE KATE MERCER FILES

D. L. MADDOX

## NOVELS BY D.L. MADDOX

The Kate Mercer Files: A Conspiracy Thriller Series

*The Super*

*The Man with the Key*

*Always at Midnight*

The Dog Walker Psychological Thriller Series

*The Dog Walker: Secrets*

*The Dog Walker: Killer*

*The Dog Walker: Stolen*

*The Dog Walker: Reckoning*

*The Dog Walker: The Prequel*

# CHAPTER 1

I FINISHED MY LAST set before the sun came up.

The gym was quiet, the way it always was at this hour—no music loud enough to intrude, no one lingering between machines, no mirrors being used for anything other than alignment. That's why I came down before six. Fewer variables. Less noise.

I wiped down the bar, re-racked the weights, and moved on without checking the clock. I already knew how long I'd been there. My workouts weren't about pushing limits; they were about maintaining them. Strength. Balance. Range of motion. The things that failed first when people stopped paying attention.

I didn't train to look fit. That never interested me. I trained to stay capable. There was a difference, and I learned it early—back when I still wore a uniform, and later, when I didn't, but the expectations stayed the same. If your body failed you, everything else followed. Hesitation. Injury. Mistakes.

I'd watched it happen often enough to make the routine nonnegotiable.

I finished with a short stretch, slow and deliberate. No rushing. Rushing meant skipping steps, and skipping steps was how injuries happened. When I stood, my muscles felt warm and responsive, the way they're supposed to. Ready, without being taxed. That was the point.

Upstairs, my apartment was still cool and dim. I showered quickly, letting the water run hot just long enough to loosen what the workout didn't reach. I didn't linger. Mornings were for preparation, not reflection.

Getting dressed took minutes. Slacks. A fresh sports bra. A simple top. A jacket I could take off if needed. Neutral colors. Nothing to draw attention. Nothing to suggest I was trying to be anything other than what I was. The fewer decisions I left for the morning, the better the day would go.

I clipped my AG credential to my belt, checked my phone, and locked the door behind me.

The elevator ride down to the garage was quiet, just the hum of cables and the faint smell of concrete and oil. I liked the descent. It marked the shift from private control to public order. From the parts of my life I managed on my own to the parts that ran by someone else's rules.

My Honda was where it always was. Five years old. Reliable. I bought it when I took the investigator job at the Attorney General's office. I always got a new car when I took a new job. It helped me mark the transition.

When I was twenty-three and graduated from the academy, I bought a used Ford Crown Victoria. I kept it for eight years—through patrol, night shifts, and the kind of calls that stayed with you, whether you wanted them to or not. When I made detective, I traded it in for a dark blue Chevy Malibu. I kept that one seven years, until I left PPD and joined the AG's office.

Now I had the Honda. Quiet. Dependable. Easy to forget until you needed it. I wondered, not for the first time, how long I'd keep this one.

I pulled out of the garage, headed west, then turned south onto Central. The city was still half asleep. Central Avenue was already filling in—office lights coming on, commuters moving with purpose, the light rail gliding past on its fixed line. Everything in its place. Everything moving the way it was designed to.

I went over the meeting in my head as I drove. Not the conclusions—those could wait—but the order. What to lead with. Where to slow down. What questions I'd be likely to get and how to answer them without overreaching. I wouldn't be accusing anyone. Wouldn't be speculating. I'd be presenting patterns that didn't make sense yet and asking for permission to keep looking.

That was the job.

The parking structure at North Central swallowed the car in a wash of concrete and shadow. I parked using my state-issued permit and followed the familiar route inside, badge out, unhurried. Security was present and unmistakable, but familiar. Systems worked best when they faded into the background for those who belonged—and announced themselves boldly to those who didn't.

Inside, the building felt the way it always did—controlled, professional, quietly authoritative. I belonged there. I'd earned that.

I reviewed my notes one last time before the meeting. Funding streams. Recipient lists. Gaps that shouldn't exist. Money that kept moving after people disappeared. I kept my language clean. Discrepancies. Anomalies. Patterns worthy of review.

I made my way through the office and took the elevator up to the executive floor—past glass walls, low voices, the steady movement of people who knew where they were going—to my supervisor's door. The placard beside it read: Assistant Attorney General, Section Chief for Financial Crimes. I knocked once and stepped inside.

Michael Hayes looked at me for a beat too long before he motioned for me to sit down. I clocked it and moved on. Men have been doing that since the academy—reacting to how I looked before they bothered to notice what I could do.

Hayes was in his late thirties, four or five years younger than me. Law school clean. Fast-track clean. The kind of man who'd learned the system by moving through it quickly instead of being ground down by it. Lawyers rose fast here. Investigators took the long road. He sat across from me with his jacket off, sleeves rolled just enough to signal approachability, his attention finally where it belonged.

"What do you have?" he asked.

I slid the folder across the table, not rushing. "State housing and care funds. Multiple programs. The recipients disappear, but they stay on the rolls, and the payments continue."

"That's not unusual," he said, reflexively.

"Except the payments are rerouted from the personal accounts," I said.

He looked up, then buried his head in my report.

Flipped through the pages, slower now. I let the silence do its work.

"I've tracked the money to a bank here in Phoenix," I continued. "Local accounts. Still active. I want account statements."

Hayes looked up. "You're asking for a warrant."

"I'm asking for access," I say. "Statements. Nothing more. I don't need motive yet. I need confirmation."

He studied me for a moment, reassessing. Whatever he thought he saw when I walked in had shifted. Good.

"And you're confident this isn't administrative noise," he said.

"Yes."

He nodded once. Not agreement. Assessment. Then: "All right. Draft the request. Keep the scope tight."

"I will."

He pushed the folder back toward me. "Bring me what you find."

I gathered the papers, already moving on. That was enough. More than enough.

I left the meeting focused and validated, already planning next steps—warrants, subpoenas, tracing the flow forward instead of backward.

There was nothing about the morning that suggested it would be anything other than routine.

Those were always the days that changed things.

# CHAPTER 2

I STEPPED INSIDE AND let the door close behind me before I moved any farther. The bank didn't announce itself. No logo on the wall. No mission statement etched into glass. If you didn't already know what this place was, you might mistake it for a private office suite or a boutique hotel that catered to people who didn't like to wait.

The space was wide and deliberately sparse. Stone floors polished to a soft sheen. Glass walls that divided without enclosing. Muted colors—gray, sand, a pale shade of blue that felt chosen more for psychology than aesthetics. Sound was dampened, absorbed. Even my footsteps seemed to know better than to echo.

There were no teller windows. No lines. No screens flashing numbers. Money didn't move here in public. It was handled somewhere else, behind doors that didn't open unless they were meant to.

At the center of the room was a reception desk, set back just far enough to create distance. Not a counter. A threshold. The kind of desk designed to slow people down, make them consider whether they were supposed to be here before they said a word.

The woman behind it looked up as I approached.

She was impeccably dressed—tailored suit, neutral colors, nothing that drew attention to itself. Her hair was pulled back neatly, makeup understated. There was no nameplate on the desk. No friendly identifier. She didn't smile, but she didn't frown either. Her expression was calm, professional, unreadable.

Her posture told me everything I needed to know. She was used to being obeyed without raising her voice. Used to people waiting for permission they didn't realize they were asking for.

I stopped a few feet from the desk, close enough to speak quietly. The distance felt intentional. Controlled.

"Good morning," she said, her tone smooth and even. Not welcoming. Not dismissive. Simply present. "How may I help you?"

I took in the room one more time before I answered. The way the furniture was arranged to discourage lingering. The lack of personal touches. The absence of anything that might suggest warmth. This wasn't a place built for convenience. It was built for discretion.

For privacy.

For control.

Whatever happened next wouldn't happen quickly. And it wouldn't happen where anyone else could see it.

I slid my credentials across the desk and kept my hand there until she took them. I didn't rush the movement. This wasn't a place that responded well to urgency.

She picked it up and looked at it carefully. Read my

name. My title. Attorney General’s Office, Investigations. She didn’t comment. Just let the information register before she set the credentials back on the desk between us, perfectly aligned with its edge.

“And how may we assist you today?” she asked.

I’m conducting a review related to state-administered housing and care programs,” I said. “I need information on several accounts held here.”

She listened without interruption. No nodding. No visible reaction. When I finished, she asked her first question.

“Are these active accounts?”

“Yes.”

“And you’re requesting transaction information?”

“That’s correct.”

She considered that, then asked another. “Is this request part of a broader review?”

“This matter is being handled internally by the Attorney General’s office,” I said.

She nodded once. The questions had been precise. Reasonable. Each one framed as clarification, not resistance. She wasn’t pushing back. She was mapping the request.

“These matters typically require internal verification,” she said. “Particularly when they involve client confidentiality.”

“I understand.”

She studied me for a moment, then looked back down at my credentials. There was no impatience in her expression. No discomfort. Just calculation.

“I’ll need to check on this,” she said finally.

Not can't. Not won't.

Just check.

"Of course," I said.

She gathered my credentials and stepped away from the desk, disappearing through a secured door behind her. The movement was smooth, practiced. This wasn't a deviation from routine. It was the routine.

I remained where I was.

Minutes passed. Five. Ten. I didn't look at my phone. I didn't pace. I stayed visible, anchored to the spot in front of the desk. People moved behind the glass walls, carrying folders, murmuring quietly to one another. No one looked in my direction for long.

Fifteen minutes in, I understood exactly what was happening.

They were waiting me out—counting on a tight schedule, on the pressure of another obligation pulling me away. If they let time slip long enough, I might have to reschedule for another day. This would give them more time to prepare.

They weren't going to deny me access. They couldn't.

All they needed was for me to run out of time.

I wasn't on a tight schedule. This was the only thing that mattered today. I could sit there as long as it took.

I stayed where I was, minus my credentials, an unresolved presence in a room designed to resolve things discreetly. They knew I wouldn't leave without them, so either the receptionist would bring them back to me, or I would go find them.

Whatever happened next, it wouldn't be accidental.

But it also wouldn't be quick.

After waiting for nearly thirty minutes, alone in the reception area, the receptionist returned without my credentials.

That told me everything before she said a word.

"I appreciate your patience," she said, stopping at the desk. Her tone was unchanged—calm, professional, carefully neutral. "Those accounts fall outside standard front-office access."

I let the sentence land. It was a familiar one. Carefully constructed. Soft enough to sound reasonable. Firm enough to end the conversation if I let it.

"I see," I said.

She watched me closely now, measuring whether I was finished. Whether I'd accept the explanation and leave quietly.

I didn't.

I reached into my bag and removed the warrant. I didn't rush. I didn't announce it. I placed it on the desk between us and slid it forward until it was impossible to miss.

"This is a lawful warrant," I said. "Failure to comply exposes your institution to contempt proceedings."

I didn't raise my voice. I didn't elaborate. The language did the work for me.

Her eyes dropped to the paper. Just for a moment. But that was enough.

Behind me, the door opened.

Footsteps. Confident. Unhurried.

Another client entered the bank.

The receptionist registered the sound instantly. Her posture didn't change, but her awareness did. She glanced past me, then back at the warrant on the desk. The calculation was immediate. A visible warrant at the front desk was a problem this institution would not tolerate.

"I'll be with you in just a moment," she said to the new arrival, her tone smooth and reassuring.

Then she turned back to me.

"If you'll follow me," she said.

It wasn't a request.

She stepped around the desk and gestured toward a secured door to the side. I gathered the warrant and moved without comment. The door opened with a quiet click, sealing the public space behind us.

Visibility issue solved.

Whatever happened next would happen somewhere private.

Exactly where they wanted it.

# CHAPTER 3

WE MOVED PAST the glass-walled offices into a corridor that looked nothing like the front of the bank. No artwork. No view. The finishes were the same—stone, wood, soft lighting—but stripped of anything decorative. This part of the building wasn't designed to impress. It was designed to disappear.

Access points clicked open ahead of us, then sealed behind us again. The effect was subtle, but cumulative. Each door narrowed the world a little further. Whatever happened back there at the reception desk was no longer my concern.

We stopped in front of a plain door with no placard, no title, no indication of who used the room. The receptionist opened it and stepped aside.

Inside, the conference room was windowless and soundless in a way that felt intentional. Thick walls. A long table. Six chairs. No phone. No visible camera. The kind of room meant for conversations that didn't leave the building.

A man was already seated at the table.

He was in his early sixties, silver hair cut short, wire-rim glasses resting low on his nose. His suit was dark and perfectly tailored, expensive without advertising the fact. He looked up as I entered, calm and unhurried, as if he'd been expecting me for some time.

My credentials were on the table in front of him.

Not tossed there. Not stacked with papers.

Placed neatly, squared to the edge, as if they had already been logged.

The receptionist closed the door behind me and left without a word.

"Ms. Mercer," the man said. His voice was measured, neutral. "Thank you for your patience."

He gestured to the chair across from him. I sat.

"I'm Richard Allen," he said. "Senior Compliance Officer."

I didn't introduce myself again. He already knew who I was.

"I understand you're conducting a review related to state-administered housing and care programs," he continued. "And that you're seeking access to certain accounts held by this institution."

"That's correct."

He nodded once, acknowledging my answer without reacting to it. His eyes flicked briefly to the warrant in my hand, then back to my face.

"Our obligation is to comply with lawful court orders," he said. "At the same time, we're required to protect client confidentiality to the fullest extent permitted by law."

"I'm familiar with the balance," I said.

"I'm sure you are," he replied. There was no

condescension in it. Just recognition. "Which is why we'll proceed carefully."

He reached forward and slid my credentials back to me. The gesture was unremarkable, but the moment wasn't. Whatever vetting needed to happen had already happened.

Then, he asked the inevitable question. "May I take a look at the warrant, Ms. Mercer?"

I pushed the document across the table, and he picked it up, studying it, flipping through the pages. After only a minute or two, he looked up at me. "I've reviewed the warrant," he said. "Its scope is specific. We intend to honor it precisely as written."

"Good," I said.

"However," he continued, folding his hands on the table, "any materials that fall outside that scope will require additional process."

"I wouldn't expect otherwise."

His gaze sharpened just slightly. Not defensive. Curious.

"You're aware that some of the accounts you've identified involve layered transfers," he says. "Multiple jurisdictions. Complex structures."

"I assumed as much," I said, not explicitly stating that all I knew, at that point, was that a number of transfers from personal accounts here in Arizona had been made to three corporate accounts at North Meridian Private Bank.

"And that offshore activity, once it leaves our institution, may fall outside our direct control."

"I'm aware of that."

A faint pause. Not resistance. Calibration.

"Then we're aligned," he said at last. "We'll begin with the records tied directly to your warrant."

This wasn't compliance offered.

It was compliance contained.

And as I watched him reach for the laptop at his side—already prepared, already waiting—I understood something else just as clearly.

They didn't scramble when I walked in.

They adjusted.

And whatever this led to, it wouldn't be the first time they'd been involved in an investigation like this. They'd been here before.

I already knew what I was looking for before the screen came on.

Arizona Emergency Support Services wasn't a typical housing authority. It was a safety net—short-term money meant to keep people from slipping all the way through. Emergency assistance. Transitional payments. Rent money meant to buy time while someone figured out their next move.

The AESS funds were deposited directly into individual accounts. Monthly. Automatic. Light oversight by design. AESS was built for speed, not permanence.

That's why it took me a while to see the pattern.

I found several people linked to these accounts who simply vanished. Stopped answering their phones. Didn't move out but never came home. Literally, dropped out of existence. But the deposits didn't stop. And at first, neither did the rent payments to the property management companies.

Then those stopped too.

What replaced them was quieter. Cleaner. Money moving where it had no reason to go. To corporate accounts at North Meridian Private Bank.

Richard Allen, the Senior Compliance Officer for North Meridian, sat across from me, his hands folded, waiting.

“What accounts would you like to begin with?” he asked.

“You read the warrant,” I said. “But if you don’t remember the accounts named, I’ve written them down here.”

I slid a sheet of paper across the table. Three names. Three corporate entities. All domestic. All already familiar to me, albeit littered with nominee directors who had nothing to do with the running of the companies.

“These,” I said. “Transaction summaries for the past twelve months.”

He glanced at the list, then turned to the computer at his side. A few keystrokes. The screen between us came alive.

The first account populated.

Rows of deposits scrolled past—hundreds of them. Different names. Different originating banks. Each one small enough to look insignificant on its own.

Together, they formed a rhythm.

I didn’t react. I didn’t comment. I just watched.

“Would you like totals?” Allen asked.

“Yes.”

The numbers appeared at the bottom of the screen. They added up to a lot of money. Millions. High enough that I already knew the other two would look the same.

He brought up the second account.

More of the same. A different shell. A different corporate name. Identical behavior.

The third confirmed it.

Hundreds of individual accounts moving government money to three corporate funnels. Money that was supposed to be used to pay their rent. Except all of these people were gone, no longer living at the approved facilities.

"Now I'd like to see outgoing transfers," I say.

He didn't hesitate. Another screen. Another shift in the data.

All three accounts routed funds to the same destination.

The money was going to a foundation in Luxembourg: Fondation Horizon Civique.

That was different.

In my line of work, outbound wires like this usually landed somewhere designed to disappear — the British Virgin Islands, Cayman, jurisdictions built on opacity. Luxembourg wasn't that. It was regulated. European. Respectable.

Which meant one of two things.

Either it was legitimate.

Or it was sophisticated.

If the money was leaving Arizona for Luxembourg, I was past the point of handling it alone. That was federal territory. I'd need the Feds to subpoena where it went next.

Because foundations don't just sit on capital.

They move it.

Allen watched my face carefully now.

"Once funds are transferred outside the country," he said, almost casually, "they fall beyond this institution's domestic jurisdiction."

I nodded, as if he'd told me something I didn't already know.

Offshore transfers didn't just complicate things. They changed who owned the problem.

Federal jurisdiction.

Different agencies. Different thresholds. Different rules.

I didn't say any of that out loud.

"I need PDFs and printouts of the transaction files for these three accounts," I said. "Twelve months. Incoming and outgoing."

He inclined his head. "We'll prepare those for you."

This wasn't the end of the money trail—but it was enough.

The pattern was real. The convergence was real. And whatever this was, it was never meant to stay local.

By the time I left North Meridian Private Bank, I didn't need to look at the records again.

I already had what mattered.

Arizona Emergency Support Services was still paying individuals tied to state-approved housing facilities—people who no longer lived there. All of them had simply disappeared. Yet, on paper, they were still recipients.

The money kept coming.

What changed wasn't the deposit. It was the destination.

Funds that once paid rent now moved into three corporate accounts at North Meridian—entities with no connection to housing, no obvious purpose beyond aggregation. From there, the money converged.

One offshore account.

That was the design. The crime was upstream in this flow. Small amounts. Repeated endlessly. Quiet enough to avoid notice unless someone was looking for patterns instead of violations. The further downstream the money went, the cleaner it got. I'd tracked it to what could very well be a completely legitimate foundation in Luxembourg.

But that was as far as I could go. I was a state-level investigator. I could document the flow. I could show the convergence. I could prove intent through repetition.

What I couldn't do was cross the water.

To find out more about the foundation in Luxembourg, and where the money was going from there, I needed to pass the ball.

Offshore accounts weren't subject to state subpoenas. They didn't respond to polite requests. They required federal reach, international cooperation, and time—none of which I controlled.

The FBI did.

If they could penetrate that account, the whole thing

would collapse. Every shell. Every transfer. Every name hiding behind a numbered entity.

It wouldn't be easy. Nothing about this would be.

But it would end it. So my plan was to bring in the FBI, make them part of the team. While they worked on the money flow, I would begin peeling back the layers at AESS itself, looking for signs of wrongdoing. Hopefully, when we were done, all the perpetrators would go to jail. And end this.

I stepped out into the clear January Phoenix sun, the city moving around me as if nothing had changed. Cars passed. People walked. The system hummed along, doing exactly what it was built to do.

Somewhere inside it, people were gone. Missing.

But the money knew exactly where to go.

# CHAPTER 4

I WALKED INTO THE Attorney General's office expecting momentum.

Not applause. Not validation. Just the next step—clean, procedural, inevitable. The kind of meeting where jurisdiction gets handed off, timelines get clarified, and the machinery of enforcement grinds forward exactly as designed.

I had already mapped it out on the drive over.

The offshore account pushed the case out of state reach. That wasn't a problem; it was a threshold. Federal jurisdiction meant resources, leverage, and the ability to follow the money past polite resistance. The FBI would take time, but time was acceptable when it came with authority.

I rode the elevator up with my posture neutral, my breathing steady. No adrenaline. No doubt.

This was what the system was for.

The executive floor was quieter than usual.

Not empty—just muted. Conversations softened as I passed. A printer whirred and stopped. Someone seated behind a glass wall stared too intently at their screen, fingers hovering over a keyboard without typing. It wasn't tension exactly. It was order—tightened.

Michael Hayes's door was open when I reached it.

"Kate," he said, standing as I entered. He smiled, warm and professional. "Thanks for coming up."

I took the chair across from his desk without ceremony. His office looked the same as always—glass walls, clean surfaces, nothing personal beyond a framed diploma and a desert landscape print that felt chosen by committee. Even the blinds were angled just so, allowing light without exposure.

"I wanted to brief you before I loop in the Bureau," I said, already opening my notebook. "The offshore transfers put this beyond our reach. I can prepare a summary and—"

"Before we get into next steps," Hayes said smoothly, "I want to say you did solid work on this."

I paused.

Praise from Hayes was rare. He wasn't withholding by nature, just efficient. Compliments, when they came, usually followed results—not conversations.

"Thank you," I said, cautious now.

"You identified a pattern no one else caught," he continued. "Clean analysis. Tight documentation. Exactly what we needed at this level."

Needed.

Past tense.

I waited.

Hayes folded his hands on the desk. When he spoke again, he didn't look at me right away. His gaze drifted to the folder aligned with the desk's edge, to the corner of the room, anywhere but my face.

"That said, bringing in the FBI won't be necessary."

The sentence landed softly. Too softly.

"I'm not sure I understand," I said.

"We've reviewed the material," he said. "The matter is being handled."

"Handled how?"

"Elsewhere."

I leaned back slightly, recalibrating. "Michael, the funds leave domestic jurisdiction. Once they hit the offshore account, we're done. We don't have subpoena power—"

"I'm aware of the limitations," he said evenly.

"Then you know escalation isn't optional. It's structural."

He nodded, as if agreeing with a point already resolved. When he finally met my eyes, it was brief—measured—like contact made to satisfy a requirement rather than invite response.

"You've done what we needed you to do."

That phrasing again.

I closed my notebook slowly. "What does that mean?"

"It means your involvement ends here."

I studied his face, searching for irritation, discomfort—anything that would suggest this was personal or reactive. There was nothing. He looked calm. Prepared.

"This case is no longer yours," he said.

I must admit, I didn't see that coming.

"If the case is being reassigned," I said, "I need to

know where it's going. To make sure the information I've gathered is transferred seamlessly."

"That information isn't necessary for you to proceed."

"Proceed with what?"

Hayes reached into a folder and slid a thin packet across the desk.

It stopped inches short of my hand. Too deliberate to be casual. The edges were crisp, untouched, like it had been waiting. I noticed there was no cover memo. No explanation. Just instructions.

Someone had already decided I didn't need context.

"You're being reassigned," he said.

I didn't touch the packet.

"To what?"

"A compliance review," he said. "Hospital billing irregularities. Narrow scope. Time-sensitive."

I stared at the packet. "You're moving me from an international diversion of government funds, involving missing persons, to a hospital audit."

"The assignment requires discretion and experience."

"That's not an answer."

"It's the assignment."

That was when I felt the shift—not anger, not yet, but something colder. Recognition. This wasn't triage. It was removal.

"I need to finish the financial trail," I said. "At minimum, I need to notify federal partners."

Hayes's tone firmed by a degree. Not sharp. Just closed.

"You are not to contact federal agencies regarding this matter."

The words were precise. Rehearsed.

"On whose authority?" I asked.

He met my gaze without blinking. "Mine."

"That's insufficient," I said. "This crosses jurisdictional boundaries."

"The decision has been made."

"What changed?"

Nothing in his expression moved. "Our needs."

Silence stretched between us. The kind that wasn't waiting for resolution—only acceptance.

"Your systems access will be adjusted," he continued, as if reading from a checklist. "Databases related to financial crimes won't be relevant to your new role."

"You're locking me out."

"We're realigning permissions."

No mention of North Meridian. No mention of offshore accounts. No mention of the bank.

The omission was the answer.

I stood. Slowly. Deliberately.

"So to be clear," I said, "I'm being reassigned, restricted, and instructed not to pursue an active financial diversion case involving state funds leaving the country."

Hayes didn't correct me.

"You're being reassigned," he said again. "Your work stands. This isn't disciplinary."

"No," I said. "It's containment."

He didn't respond.

I picked up the packet without looking at it. "If this comes back," I said, "if it explodes because someone decided not to follow it—"

"That's no longer your concern," he said quietly.

I left his office with my badge, my job, and nothing else that mattered.

By the time the elevator doors closed, I understood what had really happened.

Michael Hayes didn't have the authority to pull the plug on a case like this.

But someone up the line did.

And they were willing to sacrifice me to shut it down.

# CHAPTER 5

I'D BEEN HIKING up here ever since my mom died.

Not every week. Not on a schedule. Just often enough that the trail had become familiar in the way certain places do—through repetition, not affection. When things pressed in too tightly, I came here. When I needed distance without disappearing.

The Phoenix Mountains Preserve was close enough to reach without planning and far enough to make the city feel optional.

I parked at the trailhead just after sunrise and started up without stretching. The first incline was shallow, forgiving. Packed dirt, scattered gravel, the low brush still holding the night's cool. The city hummed behind me, present but already receding.

I set a steady pace and let my breathing find it.

Seven miles wasn't a challenge. It was maintenance. Long enough to settle the body. Long enough to keep the mind from sprinting ahead. I didn't bring music. I never did. Sound dulled things I needed sharp.

The trail climbed gradually, then tightened.

Switchbacks cut into the slope, lifting me higher above the grid. I passed a few early Saturday morning hikers—heads down, earbuds in, everyone absorbed in their own reasons for being out here. We nodded without stopping. Courtesy, not connection.

The weather was still brisk this early. January temperatures in Phoenix could drop into the forties at night, and since the sun was still coming up, the air probably hadn't reached fifty degrees yet. I was dressed for it, in layers. Jeans, hiking boots, a t-shirt, covered by a long-sleeve hiking shirt, then a sweatshirt. My daypack would receive the layers as I peeled them off, which wouldn't be long from now. When the sun got up above the mountains, it would heat things up quickly. It would probably be over seventy by the time I finished.

As I gained elevation, the city began to open up.

Office buildings. Residential blocks. Roads laid out in clean grid lines that made sense from a distance. From up here, everything looked orderly. Predictable. Systems layered over land that had never asked for them.

At the rise, I slowed.

This was the point where Phoenix spread out fully below—where the city showed itself as a whole instead of fragments. Buildings clustered around arteries of traffic. Neighborhoods stitched together by roads that promised access and control. From this angle, it all looked deliberate. Designed.

I stood there long enough for my heart rate to settle.

Then I stepped forward and dropped over the far side.

The trail narrowed immediately, slipping down into open desert. Not managed. Not groomed. Just dirt and rock, the path barely wide enough for one person, its edges crowded by jumping cholla that leaned in close, brittle and opportunistic. I adjusted my stride without thinking, careful where I placed my feet, careful where I brushed my legs, eyes alert for rattlesnakes, even though it was too early in the day for them to come out.

The city vanished behind me.

Mountains rose on all sides now, enclosing the trail in a broad, uneven bowl. The air felt heavier here, warmer, carrying the dry scent of dust and creosote. Barrel cactus dotted the slopes farther out, thick and round, their shadows short and blunt against the ground. And threaded through it all were saguaros—up to thirty feet tall, some with arms raised, others solitary and straight, rooted in rock like they'd claimed the place long before anyone thought to map it.

This was the part of the preserve that didn't pretend to be welcoming.

The trail dipped and twisted, forcing my attention downward. Loose stone slid underfoot. The ground gave just enough to punish distraction. My hiking poles came in handy on the downhill, keeping me from slipping on the dusty trail. I moved more slowly now, my body doing what it always did when the terrain demanded respect.

This was where my thinking sharpened.

I told myself the reassignment could be temporary.

Bureaucracies stalled. Reviews happened quietly. Sometimes cases went dark before resurfacing with new language and different hands. I'd seen that before. Not often, but enough to recognize the pattern.

The rationalization didn't hold.

Michael Hayes hadn't been improvising. He'd been delivering. The packet on his desk might have been assembled that morning, but the phrasing he used hadn't been chosen on the spot. The exact words had come down the ladder from above. He'd been told precisely what to say and what not to say.

And systems access didn't get adjusted unless someone had already decided I wouldn't need it again.

The trail tightened further, the cholla crowding in close enough that a misstep would leave barbs embedded in skin and fabric. I kept my arms close to my sides, shoulders squared, aware of every inch of space I occupied.

I'd spent my entire adult life enforcing the law. First in uniform. Then without it. I believed in rules—not as abstractions, but as stabilizers. Lines that mattered because people agreed to respect them. Procedure wasn't bureaucracy to me; it was restraint. It was how power stayed contained.

What happened in that office wasn't procedure.

Procedure documented decisions. It created records. It left trails.

What I'd encountered was suppression. Quiet. Clean. Designed to leave nothing behind.

Michael Hayes wasn't just blocking a case. He was taking on risk of his own.

I couldn't yet see what justified that kind of risk—but I knew it had to matter.

I climbed steadily, sweat gathering at my temples, my breathing deep and even. The physical effort kept my thoughts from scattering. Every step required attention. Every step reinforced the same conclusion.

Doing nothing here wouldn't be neutral.

Silence wouldn't preserve the system. It would protect whoever had already bent it.

The trail crested again and opened onto a stretch of high desert, the ground falling away in soft, uneven waves. No city. No roads. Just land and sky and the slow geometry of mountains holding everything in.

I stopped and looked out.

The desert didn't care about jurisdiction. It didn't recognize authority or hierarchy or the careful language people used to justify decisions made elsewhere. It existed on its own terms, indifferent and enduring.

That was when the clarity settled.

The law didn't correct itself.

It never had.

People did.

I didn't know what that meant yet. I didn't have a plan. I wasn't ready to act.

But I was done pretending that obedience and justice were the same thing.

I turned back toward the trailhead and started down, my steps measured, my breathing steady, the cholla still crowding close on either side.

Not resolved.

But no longer restrained.

# CHAPTER 6

MONDAY MORNINGS AT the office were usually quiet in a reassuring way. Predictable. The building waking up slowly, systems coming online, people easing into their roles. I liked arriving early for that reason. It gave me time to settle before the day started demanding things.

My office looked exactly the way I'd left it on Friday. Chair tucked in. Blinds half-open. A neat stack of folders on the credenza that had nothing to do with me anymore.

On my desk, a cup of coffee from the cafeteria steamed faintly, the lid already cooling. Beside it sat a small plastic container with cut fruit and yogurt—something I'd grabbed out of habit more than hunger. I didn't touch either.

Centered in front of me was the manila folder.

The hospital case.

I stared at it longer than I should have. Long enough to be aware of the sounds beyond my door: footsteps moving down the hall, a phone ringing somewhere and being answered, the low murmur of two voices passing each other without stopping. Normal. Functional. Everything in its place.

The folder made it feel staged. Like a prop placed deliberately in the center of the frame.

I told myself it was just another assignment. Reassignments happened. Priorities shifted. That was the language we used. But this one had weight to it, a density I could feel without touching it. The reassignment made physical.

I opened the folder.

The first page was administrative. Dates. Names. A summary that tried very hard to sound neutral. By the second page, my stomach tightened.

Not shock. Not surprise.

Recognition.

The language was familiar in the worst way—coded phrases, euphemisms that smoothed over harm, references to "billing anomalies" and "procedural discrepancies" that avoided the obvious conclusion. I'd seen cases like this before. Just not here.

Not since I'd arrived at the Attorney General's office five years earlier.

Back then, I'd come in expecting to spend years working my way up, learning the internal rhythms, earning trust slowly. That hadn't happened. I'd moved fast. Too fast, some people thought. Promoted to Senior Investigator after two years. Given files others avoided. Trusted to handle complexity without supervision.

I'd believed that meant something.

I flipped another page and felt a wave of nausea roll through me—not because the conduct described was new, but because of how carefully it was contained. The harm was real, albeit minimal. Vulnerable people reduced to line items. Accountability buried under compliance language. This wasn't an investigation meant to expose wrongdoing. It was meant to absorb it. To neutralize it.

This was what they wanted me doing now.

I closed the folder without finishing it and leaned back in my chair, eyes on the ceiling for a moment, letting the feeling settle instead of pushing it away. My coffee sat untouched. The steam was gone.

The contrast was unmistakable. On Friday, I'd been following a financial trail that led offshore—state-linked funds leaving the jurisdiction, structures designed to disappear into complexity. On Monday, I was holding a file designed to go nowhere.

Offshore activity didn't belong to the state. It never had. The moment funds crossed that boundary, it became a federal matter. That wasn't a gray area. It was foundational.

Remaining silent now wouldn't just be obedience. It would be withholding material information. Participating in suppression by default.

I thought about the directive Hayes had given me. Clear. Polite. Final.

Do not pursue the financial trail further.

Do not contact federal agencies.

At the time, I'd registered it as a boundary. Now I understood it for what it was.

If this was the work I was being steered toward—contained cases, neutralized outcomes—then my trajectory here was already over. Whether I stayed or not was almost beside the point. The decision in front of me wasn't about preserving my position.

It was about whether silence counted as a choice.

I looked at the folder again, then at my phone. I didn't feel panicked. I felt precise. Narrowed. The kind of clarity that comes when options fall away.

I wasn't going to leak anything. I wasn't going to make noise. I wasn't going to dramatize it.

I was going to place the information where it legally belonged.

I picked up the phone and opened the directory, scrolling until I found the number.

A legitimate channel. Financial crimes. Federal jurisdiction.

I wouldn't do this anonymously.

Not emotionally.

Deliberately.

I closed my office door before making the call.

Not because I expected anyone to listen—walls here were thick, and no one lingered this early—but because I needed the room to feel contained. I sat down, aligned the papers on my desk without reading them, and dialed the number I'd pulled from the internal directory for federal financial crimes referrals.

It rang twice.

"Financial Crimes, Phoenix Field Office," a man said. Calm. Unhurried. "This is Special Agent Miller."

"My name is Kate Mercer," I said. "I'm a Senior Investigator with the Arizona Attorney General's Office."

There was a pause—not surprise, just acknowledgment.

"How can I help you, Ms. Mercer?"

"I'm calling to flag a financial structure that exceeds state jurisdiction," I said. "It involves state-linked funds moving offshore."

"Go on."

I laid it out cleanly. No adjectives. No speculation. Just the structure: the accounts, the transfers, the timing. I explained how the money moved, where it landed, and why it could no longer be touched by state authority.

He didn't interrupt.

When I finished, he asked, "You're saying the originating funds were state-controlled?"

"Yes. By AESS."

"Where's it landing?" he asked.

"First, it goes to three corporate accounts here in Phoenix. But then it moves to Luxembourg," I said. "Entity called Fondation Horizon Civique."

"Foundation?"

"That's what it says."

"And you're sure it's not just a routing address?"

"I'm sure the money isn't staying in Arizona."

Another pause. I could hear paper shifting on his end, the faint tap of keys.

"Luxembourg," he said finally, "That's interesting."

I kept my voice steady. "Is this currently under federal review?" I asked.

"I can't speak to active matters," he said.

I felt the room narrow.

"I was instructed not to pursue the financial trail further," I said. "Or to contact federal agencies."

That got his attention. Not in tone—his voice didn't change—but in pacing.

"Who instructed you?" he asked.

"My supervisor."

"Understood."

He didn't ask for a name.

"What would you recommend?" I asked.

Another pause. Longer this time.

"I recommend you document what you have," he said. "And ensure your records are preserved."

"I have."

"Good." A beat. "You should also be aware that once information crosses jurisdictions, it tends to surface eventually. Sometimes unevenly."

"I'm aware."

"I'm sure you are."

He asked two more questions—technical, precise. I answered them. When there was nothing left to add, he said, "Thank you for bringing this to our attention."

Not reporting. Not referring. Attention.

"You're welcome," I said.

The line went dead.

I didn't move right away.

Nothing in the room had changed. My phone sat where I'd left it. The folder on my desk remained unopened. Outside my door, I could hear voices, the ordinary sounds of a workday beginning.

But the information no longer belonged solely to this office.

The call itself was a record now.

Whatever happened next would happen whether I was invited into it or not.

I picked up my phone, shut off the screen, and sat back in my chair.

I had crossed the line.

And there was no stepping back over it.

# CHAPTER 7

I SPENT THE NEXT two days moving through the hospital case on autopilot—making calls, setting up appointments—but I never left my office.

I was waiting for the hammer to fall.

It did on Wednesday afternoon.

The email came just after two. No subject line. A request to come upstairs. It didn't say now, but it didn't need to. I shut down my computer, straightened the hospital file, and took the elevator without bringing anything with mc.

The car stopped twice on the way up. Each time, the doors opened to silence and closed again. No one got on. The mirrored wall reflected back a version of me that already looked removed—badge clipped to my belt, jacket folded over my arm, nothing in my hands. I noticed a scuff near the baseboard that I was fairly sure hadn't been there before. Or maybe it had. I just hadn't been looking.

Hayes was already seated when I walked in. HR was there too—someone I recognized but had never worked with directly. A legal pad sat centered on the table. A manila folder rested on top of it, aligned carefully with the edge.

"Thanks for coming up, Kate," Hayes said. His tone was calm, almost apologetic. He didn't meet my eyes as he gestured to the chair across from him. I sat.

This wasn't a meeting. It was an execution.

Hayes folded his hands, unfolded them, then aligned the legal pad again before speaking. "We've been reviewing things internally," he said. "And we've decided this isn't working anymore."

I waited.

"There's been a loss of confidence," he continued, after a pause that felt memorized. "Not related to performance metrics. This is about fit."

Still nothing about my work. Nothing about the reassignment. Nothing about the call.

The HR representative slid the folder toward me. "This outlines the terms of your separation."

Inside was a confidentiality agreement and a severance summary.

Six months.

I kept my expression neutral, but something inside me went very still. Six months didn't happen here. I'd watched people get walked out with two weeks and a benefits pamphlet. Sometimes not even that. Investigators didn't get cushions. We got conclusions.

Six months wasn't courtesy. It was risk mitigation.

They weren't easing me out. They were buying something.

I scanned the NDA. Duration: indefinite. Scope: broad

enough to swallow the case whole. Then the Remedies section.

Injunctive relief. Liquidated damages.

I didn't need to look those up. Injunctive relief meant they could shut me down the moment I crossed the line—no warning, no drawn-out fight. Liquidated damages meant the price of breaking the agreement was already set. They wouldn't have to prove harm. They'd only have to prove I'd spoken.

Buried beneath that was the clawback language. Breach meant repayment of the severance. Then damages. Then attorney's fees. The money wasn't mine. It was conditional. Temporary. A loan that came due the instant I stopped complying.

"This is standard," the HR rep said, which told me it wasn't.

I thought about my checking account. About how thin it was. About the money I'd once had and no longer did.

My mother's illness had come fast. About a year after I'd started here. She'd been fifty-nine. Too young for Medicare. She'd never bought private insurance. We'd told ourselves we'd figure it out.

We hadn't.

I'd spent everything trying to keep her alive. Savings first. Then my retirement money. I'd known about the penalties. I'd paid them anyway. She'd died two years later, and I'd spent the two years since trying to rebuild something resembling a floor.

I hadn't gotten very far.

COBRA would be expensive. Rent wasn't flexible. The

401(k) still existed, but touching it again would mean bleeding out slowly instead of all at once.

I understood exactly what breaking the agreement would cost before I reached the signature page.

I signed.

Not because I believed the silence was permanent. Not because I accepted their version of events. I signed because I needed time. Because refusing would mean collapsing immediately, and that was exactly what they expected me to do.

“HR will walk you out,” Hayes said. He finally met my eyes, relief flickering there and gone.

The escort didn’t touch me. My badge chirped once at the security gate and went dead. HR explained next steps too quickly—final check, benefits, a number to call. Someone offered a box. I shook my head.

A coworker I passed in the hallway didn’t look up.

Outside, the sun was still high, the afternoon bright and indifferent. Traffic moved the way it always did. The city hadn’t noticed anything change.

But I had.

Six months bought time. It didn’t buy a future.

# CHAPTER 8

*One Year Later*

THE TRAIL CURVED west as it climbed, a pale ribbon of dust cut into the rock. I moved steadily, poles biting into the ground with each step, the rhythm familiar enough that I didn't have to think about it. The Phoenix Mountains Preserve stretched out ahead of me in towering brown ridges, creased with dry washes and scattered with saguaro that looked like watchmen posted too far apart to help one another.

It was Thursday. I only knew that because I'd looked at my phone earlier out of habit. The day itself didn't matter anymore. There was no office to go to, no meeting to miss, no weekend to anticipate. Just the trail, the heat, and the quiet discipline of putting one foot in front of the other.

I'd been up here a lot over the past year. At first, it had been a way to burn off the frustration from my fruitless job search, but recently, it had become something more basic: a way to keep my thoughts ordered. The trails didn't lie. They went where they went. You followed them, or you didn't.

When I reached the bench near the crest, I stopped. The city was just visible over the rise behind me—glass and concrete catching the sun—but in front of me, the land opened into rolling desert, empty and wide. I leaned my poles against the armrest and shrugged out of my pack.

The sandwich was wrapped in brown paper. Turkey, whole wheat, mustard. Cheap and efficient. I sat and ate it slowly, not because I was savoring it, but because that was how I rationed things now. Money. Food. Time.

A year earlier, I'd walked out of the Attorney General's office with six months of severance and a stack of documents that had told me everything I needed to know about how much trouble I was in. I'd made it last as long as I could. Careful spending. No trips. No new clothes. I'd canceled subscriptions, sold a few things I didn't need. I'd told myself that once I was back in the workforce, it wouldn't matter.

I hadn't gotten back in.

The first applications had gone out to federal agencies. Financial crimes units. Oversight offices. Places that dealt in the kind of work I'd been trained to do. A few of them had even called me. I'd sat in my apartment with my phone pressed to my ear, answering questions, walking them through my background, the kind of cases I'd handled.

Then nothing.

Emails that said they'd decided to move forward with

other candidates. Voicemails that never came. Silence where there had been interest.

I'd moved down a level and tried state agencies next. Other attorneys general. Regulatory departments. Anything with an investigative arm. It was the same pattern: initial engagement, polite curiosity, then a quiet closing of doors. One recruiter had sounded almost embarrassed when she told me the position had been put on hold.

I knew what that meant.

Eventually, I started calling people I used to work with. Old contacts from Phoenix PD. A lieutenant I'd once trusted. A captain who'd been at my farewell lunch when I left for the AG's office. Their voices had changed when they heard my name. Not hostile. Just careful.

Paradise Valley PD had been the low point. I'd filled out the application online, staring at the screen as I typed in my employment history. Paradise Valley was where cops went when they wanted quiet shifts and traffic tickets. No real crime. No real investigations. The fact that even they hadn't called me back had been almost funny, in a bleak, sideways way.

Private sector security hadn't been any better. Corporate risk management. Loss prevention. Compliance. The rejections there came with a different tone—overqualified, not the right fit—but the result was the same. Even the night watch jobs dried up after a few conversations. Interviews that seemed to go well and then vanished.

It hadn't taken me long to see the pattern. The language was always the same. The pauses. The way interest cooled in midair. Nobody said the word, but I knew it as surely as I'd known when a suspect was lying to me.

Blacklist.

The severance was gone now. So were my savings. The credit cards were nearly maxed. Rent was overdue. The notice taped to my door was polite, the way institutions always are when they're about to push you out.

I finished the last bite of my sandwich and folded the paper carefully, tucking it back into my pack. The desert wind moved through the low scrub, carrying the faint scent of dust and creosote. A hawk circled overhead, riding a thermal I couldn't see.

Tomorrow, I had an interview at the local Home Depot.

I'd filled out the application two nights earlier, sitting at my kitchen table with the overhead light buzzing faintly. Cashier. Stock associate. Whatever they had. It wasn't defeat. It was logistics. Work was work. Pride didn't pay rent. I doubted the invisible arms keeping me from getting work reached that low.

My phone vibrated on the bench beside me.

The number wasn't one I recognized. I let it ring once before answering.

"Kate Mercer."

"Ms. Mercer, this is Eric Westbridge from Westbridge Property Management. I'm calling regarding your application."

For a moment, I had no idea what he was talking about. Then I remembered the late-night form I'd filled out weeks ago, the one I'd almost closed before submitting. Building superintendent. A Hail Mary I hadn't expected to hear back on.

"Yes," I said. "I remember."

"We've reviewed your materials," he continued. His voice was neutral, professional. "And we think your skill set could be a uniquely good fit for one of our properties."

A good fit. The phrase landed strangely in my ear.

"Which property?" I asked.

"There are a few details we'd go over in person," he said. "We were hoping to schedule an interview."

"When?"

"Tomorrow, if that works for you."

I looked out over the desert. The trail dropped away in front of me, narrow and winding, disappearing into the folds of the hills.

"Tomorrow works," I said.

We set a time. He thanked me and hung up.

I sat there for a moment after the call ended, phone still in my hand. I didn't feel triumphant. I didn't feel relieved. Just the awareness that a quiet, unexpected opening had appeared.

I slid the phone back into my pocket, shouldered my pack, and picked up my poles. The trail was still there, waiting.

I stepped back into it and kept going.

# CHAPTER 9

I WALKED INTO WESTBRIDGE Property Management like I was walking back into my old life.

The building sat off Camelback Road in the clean, expensive part of town—glass, steel, desert landscaping clipped so precisely it looked artificial. The kind of office you rented when you wanted tenants and investors to believe you were stable. The kind of place that made people lower their voices without being asked.

Inside, the air changed. Cooler. Filtered. A faint citrus-cleaner smell that tried too hard. The lobby was quiet in the way government offices were quiet: not peaceful, controlled. A long white counter, a single vase of pale flowers, a flat-screen mounted to the wall looping a slideshow of smiling buildings and stock phrases—COMMUNITY, SERVICE, EXCELLENCE—like a hymn.

I gave my name to the receptionist.

She looked up with a practiced smile that didn't reach her eyes. Early twenties. Perfect eyeliner. A headset that made her look busier than she was.

"Katherine Mercer?"

"Kate," I said.

Her fingers moved over the keyboard. Click. Click. A pause as if the system needed time to decide what I was allowed to be.

"Yes. They're expecting you." She said. Not warm. Not unfriendly. Procedural.

I stood there holding the strap of my bag, feeling the weight of my résumé inside it like a relic. For a second, I had the ridiculous thought that if I turned around and walked out, the last year would rewind. I'd step back into my apartment, only a few blocks from here, back into a life where my name still meant something.

Instead, I watched the receptionist glance past me—toward the glass doors, toward the street—as if checking whether anyone had followed.

"Can I get you anything? Water? Coffee?" she asked.

"No. I'm fine."

She nodded, almost relieved. She didn't offer a seat. She didn't ask me to sign in. There was no clipboard, no visitor badge. No small rituals that made the waiting harmless.

Minutes passed anyway.

I took a chair along the wall, legs crossed, posture straight, the way I'd learned to sit in conference rooms when I was junior and trying to look like I belonged. I studied the space the way I studied a scene—because I couldn't help it.

A framed photo of a mid-rise building with palm trees and a caption that read THE LARKSPUR. Another that read THE FOOTHILLS. There were no names I recognized, and that was the point. The buildings didn't have personality. They had branding.

On the far wall, a plaque: WESTBRIDGE PROPERTY MANAGEMENT.

Westbridge.

A name that sounded like money and bridges and permanence.

My phone vibrated once in my pocket. A spam call. I ignored it.

The receptionist's fingers kept moving. Her screen stayed angled away from me. Once, I caught a word in the reflected glass: Mercer.

Not my first name. Not Kate.

My last name.

I swallowed and looked away before she could notice I'd noticed.

At the AG's office, those kinds of screens had been mine. Case numbers. File paths. Access permissions. Names that unlocked doors or closed them.

I'd spent years believing that if you did your job cleanly, you were safe.

Then I'd been reassigned like a piece of furniture.

Then fired with a severance package that wasn't a severance package. It was hush money.

I shifted in the chair, feeling the familiar, slow tightening in my chest—the feeling that used to hit right before a confrontation. My body remembered even if my life didn't.

This is just an interview, I told myself.

The lie landed hollow.

A door opened somewhere behind the reception counter. Quiet footsteps. A woman appeared in the hallway—tall, neat, hair pulled back so tightly it looked like it hurt.

I didn't know her name yet, but I knew the type. I'd sat across from women like her in conference rooms and watched them dismantle other people without raising their voices.

Her eyes landed on me and held.

Then she smiled.

It was small. Polite. The smile of someone who had practiced smiling in front of lawyers.

"Ms. Mercer," she said.

Her voice was calm, low, and perfectly controlled.

I stood.

"Kate," I corrected automatically.

The woman's gaze flicked—just once—toward the receptionist, like a silent reminder that she was supposed to be doing something better than watching.

"Of course. Kate." She stepped forward, extending her hand. "I'm Elaine Westbridge. Thank you for coming in."

I kept my eyes on hers and shook her hand. Her grip was moderate; I softened mine accordingly.

Up close, she looked like someone who didn't sleep deeply. Her skin was smooth, makeup minimal, but there was a tension at the corners of her mouth that didn't belong on a woman who ran a successful company. Her outfit was expensive in a muted way—a blazer that didn't wrinkle, a blouse that didn't cling. Nothing shiny. Nothing loud. No jewelry except a thin watch that looked more like a tool than an accessory.

"Right this way," she said.

The receptionist didn't move.

Elaine Westbridge led me past the counter and into the office.

The hallway was lined with glass-walled rooms, the kind that promised transparency while giving you none. Inside, employees sat at their desks like they were pretending to work for someone important. Some looked up. Most didn't. A few glanced at me and then looked away fast, as if eye contact was a decision with consequences.

No one smiled.

No one frowned.

They held their faces blank.

The fluorescent lights were softened by diffuser panels, but the air still had that office hum—the low vibration of machines and ventilation and people trying to be quiet. Somewhere a phone rang twice and stopped. A printer whirred. A door closed. A muted laugh that cut off too quickly.

Elaine walked at a steady pace, not fast enough to seem anxious, not slow enough to invite conversation. She didn't look back to see if I was following. She assumed I was.

That assumption made my skin prickle.

At the end of the hallway was a conference room with frosted glass. The kind of frosting that made you visible as a shadow. The kind that turned people into shapes.

Elaine Westbridge opened the door.

Inside, a man stood up.

Mark Westbridge.

He was in his mid-fifties, dressed well but not as tightly as Elaine. His tie was slightly crooked, like he'd adjusted it in a hurry and then forgotten. His smile was wider than it needed to be, warm in a way that felt forced.

"Kate," he said, stepping forward with both hands open as if he were greeting someone at a family dinner. "Thank you for coming." Somehow, he'd gotten word that I preferred Kate to Ms. Mercer.

His handshake lingered half a second longer than Elaine's. A human touch. A plea.

Behind him, the conference room table was set like a presentation. A folder in front of each chair. A carafe of water. Three glasses already poured.

"Please," Mark said. "Have a seat."

I sat.

Elaine sat across from me, posture straight, hands folded. Mark sat beside her at an angle—slightly turned toward me, as if he wanted to be my ally inside his own meeting.

A wall-mounted screen behind them showed the Westbridge logo. The same clean font I'd seen in the lobby. The same lie of stability.

Elaine opened her folder.

I didn't.

"Kate," Elaine began, "I'll start by saying we've reviewed your background. Thoroughly."

There it was.

Not résumé. Not experience.

Background.

My throat tightened.

Mark leaned forward. "We're impressed. Your time with Phoenix PD, then the Attorney General's office—Senior Investigator after two years. That doesn't happen."

No. It didn't.

It happened to people who got results.

And then it stopped happening when those results made the wrong people nervous.

I kept my face neutral.

"Thank you," I said.

Elaine nodded once, as if checking a box.

"Our firm manages a portfolio of residential properties across the valley," she said. "A range of asset classes."

Asset classes.

Not buildings. Not homes.

Mark jumped in. "We're looking for someone with judgment. Someone steady. Someone who can manage... situations."

Elaine's eyes flicked to him, almost imperceptible. A correction without words.

Mark's smile tightened and then reset.

"What kind of situations?" I asked.

Elaine's gaze didn't waver. "Tenant issues. Rent irregularities. Complaints. The usual things that can arise in a building with a high volume of residents."

That was a lot of words to say nothing.

"In one building in particular," Mark added quickly, "we've had... some disruptions."

Disruptions.

Not evictions. Not crime. Not violence.

Just disruptions.

I waited.

Silence stretched. Elaine didn't fill it. Mark looked like he wanted to.

I let the silence sit because I'd learned that people

revealed more when you gave them room to be uncomfortable.

Elaine finally said, “We need oversight on-site.”

“And you’re looking for a superintendent,” I said.

Mark nodded. “Yes. A resident superintendent. Someone who can oversee maintenance, coordinate vendors, keep eyes on the place.”

Keep eyes.

He said it like a phrase he’d been told to use.

Elaine’s expression didn’t change, but something tightened in her jaw.

Mark cleared his throat. “It’s a two-hundred-unit building.”

Two hundred units wasn’t small. It wasn’t enormous either. It was big enough to disappear inside.

I kept my tone steady. “Why me?”

Mark opened his mouth.

Elaine answered.

“Because you understand systems,” she said. “Because you understand documentation. Procedure. Accountability.”

Her voice was even, but her eyes were sharp.

I felt the old anger stir—hot and quiet.

Accountability.

That word didn’t belong in a room where two people were refusing to say what was actually happening.

“You’re interviewing for a Super, right?” I asked. “Not an investigator.”

Elaine held my gaze. “We’re asking for someone we can trust.”

There it was again.

Not qualified.

Trust.

My pulse thudded once, hard.

Mark jumped in, too quickly. "And we understand your situation. We understand you've had... a difficult year."

A difficult year.

He said it like it was weather.

My fingers curled slightly under the table.

I forced my voice to stay calm. "You did a background check."

Mark's smile faltered.

Elaine didn't blink. "We did our due diligence, yes."

That was confirmation and warning in one sentence.

I took a breath and let it out slowly.

"What exactly is the building issue?" I asked.

Elaine's answer was immediate. Too immediate.

"Late payments. Tenants who are behind. Some residents who don't respond to notices. We need someone on-site to make sure the situation doesn't escalate."

"Escalate to what?" I asked.

Mark's eyes flicked—quickly—to Elaine.

Elaine's voice stayed smooth. "To legal action. To disorder. To reputational harm."

Reputational harm.

That was an AG phrase. That was a politician's phrase.

That was not a property management phrase.

I looked at the folder in front of me.

I didn't open it.

Not yet.

Mark leaned forward again. "Kate, I'll be candid.

We're offering you a package because we need someone strong. Someone who can stabilize a building."

Elaine's eyes sharpened.

Mark kept going anyway, like he couldn't stop himself. "We're prepared to offer a salary comparable to what you made at the AG."

My stomach tightened.

Comparable.

That shouldn't be possible.

"And," Mark said, "you'll have an apartment in the building. Rent-free. A very nice apartment, I might add." He smiled, his eyes twinkling with generosity.

There it was.

The hook.

My brain started doing math before I could stop it.

Eighteen hundred a month. Plus the HOA—three ninety-five. Utilities. Parking. Little fees that never stopped appearing like insects.

Two thousand four hundred. Two thousand five hundred.

Thirty thousand a year just to keep a roof over my head in a building where the gym was downstairs and the lobby had concierge smiles and no one asked questions.

Free rent wasn't a perk. It was oxygen.

I kept my face calm anyway.

"What building?" I asked.

Elaine's gaze held mine. "The Ashford."

I knew the area.

Midtown. Central Corridor. Different world.

Not where I'd chosen to live when I had a salary and a reputation. Not where you paid extra for safety. Not where you walked out at night without checking who was behind you.

It wasn't dangerous on paper.

But it wasn't my world.

"And the job is..." I began.

Elaine slid the folder across the table with two fingers, aligning it perfectly in front of me.

"Everything is outlined there," she said. "Scope. Expectations. Reporting structure."

I opened the folder.

The paper smelled new, freshly printed. The words were clean and corporate. The job description read like any superintendent role—maintenance coordination, vendor oversight, tenant relations, security interface.

But there were extra lines.

Language about documenting incidents. About reporting anomalies. About discretion.

A lot of words about discretion.

I looked up.

Elaine watched me the way she'd watched me in the lobby—as if she could see the moment my instincts shifted.

Mark gave me a hopeful smile. Or maybe it was a guilty one.

I closed the folder gently.

My throat felt tight, but my voice stayed steady. "This is a generous offer."

"Yes," Elaine said. "It is."

Mark nodded. "We want you to be able to focus on the building. Not worry about... logistics."

Logistics.

Rent. Food. Survival.

I could have walked out. I could have said no. I could have kept clinging to the last shred of pride I had left and watched it evaporate in my empty apartment when the eviction notice finally came.

And I could have told myself, again, that the system would correct itself if I just waited long enough.

It wouldn't.

I'd already learned that.

But I had also learned something else.

Telling the truth out loud got you crucified.

I was not going to walk into another institution and hand them my neck.

If something was wrong at The Ashford, I would see it for myself first.

Quietly.

Carefully.

On my own terms.

I looked at Elaine. Then at Mark.

"I can start when?" I asked.

Mark exhaled like he'd been holding his breath for a year.

Elaine's smile returned—small, controlled, almost relieved.

"Tomorrow," she said. "If that works for you."

Tomorrow.

I nodded once.

"It works. Thank you."

And as I stood to leave, I understood something I didn't want to name.

This wasn't reaching for a lifeline.

It was surrender.

# CHAPTER 10

I KNEW THE ASHFORD wasn't my kind of place the moment I saw it.

It rose above the surrounding blocks like something left behind by a different era—twelve stories of concrete and narrow windows, the color of dusted bone. Not quite derelict, not quite maintained. A building that had once been modern and now survived on momentum. It sat in Midtown Phoenix, close enough to downtown to feel the city's pulse, far enough away to be forgotten.

My old place in the Camelback Corridor had been all glass and soft lighting. A lobby that smelled faintly of citrus and money. A front desk where someone always knew your name. A gym downstairs so you never had to be seen sweating in public. Everything designed to make you feel protected from the rest of the city.

The Ashford didn't pretend to protect anyone.

The entrance doors were thick glass, scratched and cloudy, and when I pushed through them, the air inside felt heavier, like it had been used too many times. A bank of elevators sat at the far end of the lobby, their brushed metal dulled by fingerprints. A security camera blinked red in the corner, old enough that it probably recorded more static than faces.

The management office was set off to one side, behind a pane of glass that didn't quite reach the ceiling.

Mara Feldman looked up when I stepped inside.

She was in her early forties, hair pulled back too tightly, the skin at her temples smooth and shiny. A soft gray cardigan over a white blouse, slacks pressed recently enough to suggest someone still cared about appearances. Her smile came quickly, then held there like she was afraid to let it drop.

"Katherine Mercer?" she asked.

"Kate," I said.

Her fingers hovered over the keyboard before she typed, as if even small movements required permission. The monitor was angled away from me, but I could see motion reflected in the glass partition behind her—rows, columns, numbers shifting.

"Welcome to The Ashford," she said. "We're very glad you're here."

I let my eyes wander while she pretended not to notice.

A board behind her held dozens of hooks for keys—some empty, some crowded with brass and steel. A clipboard sat on the counter, unit numbers written in different inks. A thick ledger lay open beside it, marked with sticky notes in red, yellow, and blue.

Some numbers were circled.

Others crossed out.

"Do I need to sign anything?" I asked.

"Oh—no. No, that's fine." She waved it away too quickly. "We'll take care of all that later."

Later was never a comforting word.

I rested my hands on the counter and waited. Mara glanced at her screen, then at me, then back to the screen again. When she spoke, her voice dropped a notch.

"Ray will be with you in a moment. He's maintenance. He'll show you around."

"I'd like that," I said. "I want to understand the building."

"Of course," she said, nodding. "It's... big."

That wasn't what I was thinking. Old was. Layered. The kind of place that absorbed stories and didn't give them back.

Behind Mara, the ledger was still open just enough for me to catch three unit numbers written in a different hand than the rest.

They were underlined.

Mara saw me looking and snapped it shut.

Her smile returned, thin and careful.

"Coffee?" she asked.

"No thanks," I said. "I'm fine."

It wasn't true, but it was close enough.

And as I stood there, waiting for Ray to appear, I had the quiet, creeping sense that I'd stepped out of one controlled environment and into another—one that didn't bother pretending it was benign.

Ray Donnelly was just approaching the office when I stepped out to try to clear my head.

He didn't look like someone who worked in a

two-hundred-unit high-rise. He looked like someone who had been worn down by one. Late forties, maybe, with a permanent squint in his eyes as if he spent his days in dim basements and boiler rooms. His uniform shirt was clean but frayed at the cuffs, the kind of detail you only noticed when you were trained to notice things. A man who fixed what broke, but never himself.

"You the new Super?" he asked.

"Kate Mercer," I said, extending my hand.

He nodded once. Shook. No smile. "Ray. I'll show you what matters."

That was an odd way to put it, but I followed him anyway.

We moved away from the bright lobby and into the building's back corridors, where the air smelled faintly of metal and old water. Took an elevator down to the basement. The polished tile gave way to concrete. The lighting flattened everything. Pipes ran overhead like exposed veins.

"Most of the work happens down here," Ray said. "Tenants don't see it. That's how management likes it. And I like it too. My apartment's down here."

He said it like he felt safer down here. I guess he did.

We moved back up into the residential part of the building. I clocked the cameras as we passed them. Not just in the main corridors, but tucked into corners, watching service doors, stairwells, utility alcoves. Whoever had designed the system hadn't skimped.

"You have a lot of security," I said.

Ray hesitated. Just long enough to matter.

"More than we used to."

We stopped in front of a heavy metal door with a keypad. He didn't open it.

"Some units," he said, keeping his voice low, "you're not supposed to go into."

"That's not normal," I said.

He gave me a sideways look. "No. It isn't."

"Why?"

Ray shook his head. "Orders. From before you. From the last guy."

The last guy. The old Super.

"What happens if someone does?" I asked.

Ray stared at the door as if it might answer for him. "We get written up. Maybe worse."

That wasn't a property management answer. That was absolute control.

We kept walking.

That was when I saw Evan Pike for the first time.

He stood in a side corridor near the stairwell, pretending to look at his phone. Early thirties, lean, with the kind of body that came from restless energy instead of a gym. His eyes flicked up when we passed.

Not curious.

Assessing.

Ray's jaw tightened. He leaned slightly toward me as we walked past.

"Don't engage him."

"Who is he?" I murmured.

"Tenant. Apartment 109. Trouble. Always where he shouldn't be."

Evan's gaze followed us until we turned the corner.

"You think he heard that?" I asked.

Ray didn't answer.

We took an elevator up to the fourth floor. When the doors opened, the hallway was quiet—too quiet for a building this size. Carpet muted our footsteps. Doors lined both sides, identical and anonymous.

Ray stopped in front of 411.

"Thomas Keene," he said. "One of the sealed ones."

He unlocked the door.

The smell hit me first—not rot, not decay, just the stale stillness of a space that should have been occupied and wasn't. We stepped inside.

It was a one-bedroom apartment, modest but neat. Couch. Coffee table. A laptop sitting closed on the desk. A half-empty mug in the sink. Food in the fridge. Clothes in the closet.

An unmade bed.

No boxes. No suitcases. No sign of preparation.

"This man didn't move," I said.

Ray shook his head. "No. He vanished."

"How long ago?"

"Eight months."

"And no one came to clean it out. It should be rented out again."

"Wasn't allowed."

I walked through the apartment slowly, cataloging what was there the way I used to catalog crime scenes. A toothbrush. Prescription bottles. A grocery receipt still pinned to the fridge by a magnet.

This was a life paused, not ended.

"There are two more like this," Ray said quietly.

"Who pays the rent?"

"No idea. Maybe it doesn't get paid at all."

That answer opened a door I didn't yet want to walk through.

We left the apartment and locked it behind us.

Back in the hallway, Evan Pike was there again.

Different spot. Same posture. Same watchful eyes.

He didn't pretend this time.

Ray swore under his breath.

"He's not supposed to be up here," Ray muttered.

Evan's gaze slid to me and held.

Not curiosity.

Recognition.

Something cold settled in my chest.

"Let's go," Ray said, steering me toward the elevator.

As the doors closed, Evan was still standing there, staring at where I had been.

After the tour, Ray peeled off toward the service elevator without another word, already retreating back into the machinery of the building. I watched him go, then turned and walked straight for the office.

Mara looked up when I came in. Too quickly.

"Those sealed apartments," I said. "That isn't standard procedure."

Her fingers stilled on the keyboard. "No."

"Then why are they sealed?"

She hesitated, eyes flicking toward the hallway as if someone might be listening. "The last Super ordered it. Said they were off-limits."

"Why?"

Mara shook her head. “He never said. Just that it came from… above.”

“Above where?”

She didn’t answer.

I took a breath. “How do I contact him?”

Another pause. Longer this time.

“His name was Gareth Cole,” Mara said quietly. “I can give you his contact information. But that probably won’t do you much good.”

“Why?”

She met my eyes.

“Because he’s missing, too.”

# CHAPTER 11

MARA DIDN'T GIVE me time to breathe.

Because the words *he's missing, too,* were still hanging in the air—raw, final, the kind of sentence that didn't belong in a tiny office where people worried about toner cartridges and vendor invoices. I stood there with my keys in my hand, ready to leave and never come back, feeling the room tilt slightly, like my body was trying to recalibrate to a world where a person could vanish, and the building could keep functioning.

Mara was already reaching into a drawer, already moving like she could outrun what she'd just admitted.

"We should get you settled," she said.

The phrase landed wrong. Too quick. Too normal. Like she was pulling a sheet over something that hadn't cooled yet.

I didn't move.

The office around us kept breathing. A phone rang and stopped. The overhead lights buzzed with that faint electrical irritation I'd always associated with places that wanted to feel efficient and ended up feeling sterile.

Everything was the same.

Nothing was the same.

"The old Super," I said, and my voice sounded steadier than I felt. "Was I going to be staying in his apartment?"

Mara's answer came too quickly.

"No."

Not a pause. Not a blink.

"That one's sealed," she added, as if she were explaining that the copier was out of order. "The Westbridges told me not to touch it."

My stomach tightened.

So it wasn't maintenance. It wasn't procedure. It wasn't even a choice someone in the building had made in the moment.

It was policy.

It came from above.

"And where am I staying?" I asked.

Mara hesitated—just long enough for the truth to flicker through her eyes. Then she said the word like it was a bandage.

"The penthouse."

That didn't belong in this building. It sounded like skyline glass, rooftop pools, and a concierge who knew your dog's name. Not a two-hundred-unit high-rise where doors were sealed shut like tombs.

I made myself nod as if the answer didn't rattle me.

"Show me," I said.

Mara's shoulders loosened a fraction, as if movement itself was relief. She led me out of the office and down a short corridor I hadn't seen on my first pass—past a maintenance closet, past a stairwell door, past a wall where the paint had been patched and repatched as if the building had been trying to heal itself for years and never quite managed.

At the end of the corridor was a door marked AUTHORIZED ACCESS ONLY.

Mara swiped a card. The lock clicked.

Beyond it was an elevator that didn't match the rest of The Ashford's tired, practical beige. This one was brushed steel, clean enough to reflect light. The buttons glowed a soft blue. There were no floor numbers. No worn labels. No fingerprints pressed into plastic by hundreds of hands.

Just a key slot.

Mara inserted a key, and the doors parted with a soft, expensive hiss.

"This elevator doesn't stop on the regular floors," she said quietly, stepping in. "It goes straight up."

"Why?" I asked.

She hesitated. Her eyes slid away from mine, toward the closing doors, like she didn't want to be caught saying too much inside the box that carried us.

"It keeps people from wandering where they shouldn't," she said. Then, almost as an afterthought—almost as if the name slipped out before she could stop it—"And it'll keep undesirables... like Evan... away from you."

That landed harder than the missing Super.

So Evan wasn't just an annoyance. He wasn't just a tenant with an attitude problem.

He was known.

And I was already being protected from him.

The doors slid shut, and the elevator began its ascent in silence. No canned music. No cheerful voice announcing floors. Just the hum of the motor and the faint vibration under my shoes.

It felt like the building was lifting me out of its bloodstream.

I'd spent most of my adult life in structures like this—government buildings, precincts, courthouse annexes—places designed to make people feel small, designed to make them comply. I knew the sensation of being moved through a system. You entered. You waited. You sat where you were told. You spoke when permitted. You left with paperwork.

But this elevator felt different.

This felt like extraction.

Up, away from the regular floors, away from whatever lurked behind those sealed doors, away from the tenants who had to use the lobby elevators with the sticky buttons and flickering floor numbers.

I watched my reflection in the brushed steel—my face too composed, my eyes too alert. The kind of face I wore when I was trying not to show fear. The kind of face I'd worn in Michael Hayes's office, right before he slid a folder toward me and told me everything was over in the same tone someone would use to reschedule a meeting.

I hadn't expected that memory to hit me here.

But maybe that was the point.

Everything in my life had become a corridor leading to closed doors.

When the elevator stopped, the doors opened onto a hallway that didn't belong to The Ashford.

The carpet was thick enough to swallow sound. The lighting was warm, recessed, flattering. The air smelled faintly like clean linen and something expensive I couldn't name. No bleach. No stale fryer grease drifting in from someone's apartment. No undertone of mildew or old smoke.

There were only three doors on the entire floor, spaced far apart like private residences.

Mara stepped out and gestured toward the center door.

"Each unit is about three thousand square feet," she said. "This one's the center."

Three thousand.

I stared at the door, trying to picture the floor plans I'd seen in a dozen high-rises over my career. Three thousand square feet wasn't an apartment. It was a statement.

It didn't feel like housing.

It felt like an offering.

Mara unlocked the door.

Inside felt even less like The Ashford than the hallway.

The living room opened up in front of me like a magazine spread—clean lines, soft neutrals, furniture that looked heavy and expensive without trying too hard. Thick rugs. A low couch that probably cost more than my car. A kitchen with stone counters and stainless steel appliances that belonged in a luxury condo, not a building whose lobby smelled like old coffee and damp concrete.

Three large bedrooms, each one en-suite. And to top it off, one of the bedrooms had been converted into a gym with a treadmill, rowing machine, and a variety of resistance machines. Every piece of equipment in the room was something I used regularly at the gym in my apartment building uptown. The Westbridges had truly outdone themselves with their "background checks."

The lighting was deliberate—soft and layered, no harsh overhead glare. Modern art on the walls—curated, not personal. The air felt conditioned in a way that didn't just mean cool; it meant controlled.

I walked farther in, slow and careful, and my mind did what it always did. It inventoried.

No shoes by the door.

No mail on the counter.

No condensation rings on the coffee table.

No scuffs on the baseboards.

No half-empty bottle of dish soap under the sink.

No signs of a person.

Not even the faint chaos that lived in every normal home—keys in a bowl, a jacket thrown over a chair, a dent in a cushion where someone always sat.

This place wasn't lived in.

It was kept.

"The Westbridges keep this one furnished for special guests," Mara said, trying for casual. "But I guess they've decided to let you use it. Lucky you."

I turned slowly, taking it in from a different angle.

"What guests?" I asked.

Mara's smile tightened. "People visiting from out of town."

"Do they introduce them to you?" I asked.

Mara shook her head.

Her face said she was lying—or that she was telling the truth and hated it.

She handed me a key. It was heavier than it needed to be, like it belonged to a safe deposit box.

"I'll leave you to get settled," she said. "Let me know if you need help moving."

And then she was gone, the door clicking softly behind her.

I stood in the center of the penthouse, alone, and let the quiet settle around me.

In the old days—before the reassignment, before the firing, before I watched my career be folded into a manila envelope—I would have read this kind of offer as success. A reward. A sign that someone recognized my value.

But I'd learned the hard way that rewards weren't always rewards.

Sometimes they were restraints.

I walked through the apartment again, slower, letting my attention catch on details.

The pillows were too perfectly arranged.

The throw blanket had a sharp fold like it had never been used.

The fridge held bottled water and nothing else.

The closets had empty hangers lined up in neat rows, waiting.

Waiting for a person.

Waiting for a story.

I moved toward the sliding doors and stepped out onto the balcony.

It was enormous—tiled in pale stone that held the last warmth of the day. A long outdoor couch sat against one wall, cushions crisp and clean. A table big enough for eight people, with chairs that looked like they belonged at a resort. A single lounge chair positioned at an angle to the skyline, as if someone had once sat there and decided this view mattered.

I stood at the railing and looked out over Phoenix.

Downtown rose not far away—glass and steel catching the light, the towers sharp against the desert sky. The grid of streets stretched outward like a plan drawn by someone who believed order could be forced onto anything. Traffic crawled in bright lines, red and white, relentless.

From up here, the city looked clean.

From up here, you could pretend the system worked.

I found myself looking for landmarks without meaning to. The courthouse. The administrative buildings where I'd spent years believing my work mattered. Places where people wore badges and called themselves public servants and filed reports like they were prayers.

My old life was out there, still humming along, as if it had never spit me out.

I walked to the lounge chair—the one angled toward the skyline—and sat. Not because I wanted comfort. Because sitting meant I could think without pacing. Because the chair gave me a view of the city and a view back into the apartment, and my back was against the wall where no one could come up behind me.

A habit.

I let my hands rest on my knees and did the math, because my brain did math when it wanted to avoid panic.

Eighteen hundred a month in rent.

Three ninety-five in HOA.

Utilities that never stopped rising.

The little fees—parking, package lockers, amenity fees—death by a thousand paper cuts.

I'd clung to that apartment for far too long because it was safe, because the gym was downstairs, because the lobby was bright, and the doors were locked, and I didn't have to think about who might be waiting in the hallway.

But safety didn't matter if you couldn't pay for it.

I'd been three weeks away from eviction when Elaine Westbridge told me I could start tomorrow.

Three weeks away from an empty fridge and a storage unit full of furniture I couldn't afford to keep.

The apartment here wasn't a perk.

It was survival.

But it was more than that.

I sat there and stared at the skyline until the truth hardened into shape.

This wasn't generosity.

It was prepayment.

The Westbridges didn't give me this because they were kind. They gave me this because they knew what I would find. They knew I would see sealed doors and missing people and patterns that didn't belong in any building that wanted to stay alive.

So they paid me in advance.

Not to stay.

To stay quiet.

For a moment, my mind tried to offer alternatives—soft explanations, the kind you reached for when you didn't want the ugly answer.

Maybe they were terrified of lawsuits.

Maybe they'd had a violent incident and wanted someone stable.

Maybe this was just corporate paranoia.

But none of those explanations required sealed apartments.

None of them required the last Super to be missing.

None of them required a private elevator and three thousand square feet of hush money.

I closed my eyes, and another memory slid in without invitation: the beep of my badge deactivating. The way the sound was small and final, like a door locking itself behind you. The HR rep talking too fast, rehearsed. Michael Hayes aligning the severance folder precisely in front of me, as if the symmetry could make what he was doing feel clean.

I'd told the truth and been crucified.

I'd learned what happened when you made a system uncomfortable.

The old me would have confronted the Westbridges. Would have demanded answers. Would have called the police from the lobby and watched the building scramble.

That Kate was gone.

This Kate understood something now.

Systems don't protect truth.

They neutralize it.

Ray knew more than he was saying.

Mara knew more than she was saying.

Someone inside this building was feeding names to someone unknown. The Westbridges? Probably. Maybe. Maybe not.

But one thing was certain—the missing Super was proof of what happened to people who pushed.

I opened my eyes and looked back through the glass doors at the penthouse behind me—so clean it felt like a stage set.

I would move in.

I would close out my Camelback apartment.

I would take the money.

And I would not go to the authorities.

Not yet.

Because going to the authorities was how you got buried.

This time, I was going to stay employed long enough to understand what I was standing inside.

I stood up from the lounge chair and walked back into the apartment, the key heavy in my hand.

I was staying.

I was watching.

And I was going to figure out exactly what kind of machine The Ashford had become—quietly, from the inside.

# CHAPTER 12

"TELL ME ABOUT the missing tenants," I asked Mara.

The words came out flatter than I expected—like I was asking for a routine report, like this was a normal second morning on a normal job. Like I hadn't stood in this same office yesterday and learned that my predecessor was missing.

Mara's monitor glowed at her desk, casting a dim rectangle across her hands. She had that same careful look she always wore—hair in place, cardigan buttoned, posture composed—like she believed neatness could keep a building from bleeding.

"What kind of information are you looking for?" she asked.

There it was again: procedure as armor. Give me categories. Give me boxes. Don't make me say anything in plain English.

"Their names, apartment numbers, their ages, how long they've been missing, who they socialized with in the building, if they had frequent guests, that kind of thing."

Mara's fingers hovered over the keyboard for half a beat—like she was deciding whether the system would punish her for complying. Then she changed her mind and pulled open a drawer in her desk. Removed a folder. Then another. And another. And finally, a fourth folder. Paper files. Actual paper. Paper was better than nothing but it also made things easy to "misplace."

"Okay," she said softly, and began stacking the folders in front of her. "Three tenants. And... Gareth Cole."

Hearing the name out loud tightened something in my chest. The missing Super didn't feel like a case yet. He felt like a warning.

Mara slid the first file out of the stack and opened it with care, like the folder might cut her.

"Thomas Keene," she said. "Apartment 411. Mid-fifties. Missing eight months."

"Occupation?" I asked.

"Remote contractor," Mara said, scanning the intake sheet. "IT work, I think. He listed 'project-based'—no employer on file. Always paid on time. Never caused problems. No complaints. No late notices."

No late notices. No drama. No paper trail.

Mara turned a page. "He... didn't have any emergency contacts listed. That's unusual. Most people put someone, even if it's a cousin or a friend. He left it blank."

I kept my face still, but my mind did what it always did when it sensed a pattern—it started building the shape of it before I gave it permission.

"And... social?" I asked.

Mara's eyes flicked up at me, then down again

immediately. “No guests noted. No visitor parking passes logged. No noise complaints. Nothing.”

She said it like nothing was a relief. Like quiet was safety.

It wasn’t.

Mara opened the second file.

“Lila Rosen,” she said. “Apartment 318. Seventy-two. Missing thirteen months.”

Thirteen months.

The number registered, clean and clinical. Long enough to mean whatever had happened to Lila Rosen wasn’t a misunderstanding, or a delay, or a temporary vanishing. After a year, absence had long since hardened into fact.

“She was... disabled,” Mara continued, careful with the word. “Voucher tenant. Mostly stayed inside. Didn’t have a vehicle registered. Ray used to do small things for her—light bulbs, smoke detector batteries—things like that. She was... reclusive.”

“What does her file say?” I asked.

Mara stared at the screen a moment longer than necessary.

“Nothing,” she said.

“Nothing?”

She shook her head. “There’s no move-out. No transfer. No relocation. No termination. It’s just... open.”

I leaned forward. “And that means what?”

Mara swallowed. “It means, on paper, Lila Rosen never left.”

Which meant the system still believed she was alive,

still believed she was occupying that apartment, still believed the money had somewhere to go.

She slid the third file toward herself.

"Javier Morales," she said. "Apartment 506. Early thirties. Missing almost three months."

Almost three months. New enough that the fear still had sharp edges. New enough that I could almost picture him walking through the lobby and not knowing he was already being tallied.

"Occupation?" I asked.

Mara flipped a page. "He listed 'warehouse' and then a company name—temp agency. No benefits. He moved in fast. Paid his portion, but the bulk of his rent was covered by AESS. Just like the other two."

I felt my spine go rigid.

AESS.

For a second, I didn't hear the office anymore. The hum of the lights, the distant elevator bell, the muted voices down the hall—all of it went thin, like someone had turned the volume down on the world and left only one phrase in the air.

Arizona Emergency Support Services.

The program I'd lived inside for months without ever stepping foot in it.

My old case didn't come back like a memory. It came back like a door slamming open.

*January sun.*

*North Meridian's glass lobby.*

*The controlled quiet.*

*The compliance officer sliding my credentials back across the table like I was already logged.*

And then the numbers—rows and rows of deposits—small enough to look harmless, repeated enough to become a machine.

AESS wasn't a housing authority. It wasn't built for long-term oversight. It was a safety net designed for speed. Money meant to keep people upright when life buckled. Deposits meant to buy time.

And that speed—the urgency, the light oversight—was exactly why it had been vulnerable.

I'd watched those deposits keep coming even after recipients vanished from the places they were supposed to be living. I'd watched rent payments stop...and something cleaner replace them. I'd watched money shift into funnels that had no reason to exist.

I'd told the truth about it.

And the state had buried me for making the wrong people uncomfortable.

Now I was sitting in a property management office in a run-down high-rise, listening to the same acronym come out of Mara Feldman's mouth like it was a normal part of a tenant file.

My throat tightened.

Mara was still talking. "It's pretty common here," she said, not looking up. "AESS covers part or all of the rent for some residents."

I made myself breathe through my nose—slow, quiet—like I used to in interrogations when someone said something that spiked my pulse and I couldn't let them see it.

"Okay," I said, and my voice didn't sound like mine. "So... Thomas Keene, Lila Rosen, Javier Morales."

Mara nodded, relieved to be back inside the list. She didn't see what had just happened to me. Or she saw it and refused to name it.

I leaned forward slightly, lowering my voice without meaning to. "Do they have anything in common?"

Mara blinked, thrown by the question—not because she didn't understand it, but because it wasn't the kind of question she wanted to answer.

"I don't know," she said carefully. "They're... different."

"They're not," I said.

The words came out before I softened them.

Mara's eyes flicked up. I could see the instinct in her face—the instinct to deny, to smooth, to keep the air calm.

I kept going anyway, because my mind was already lining the files up like evidence on a table.

"No visitors," I said. "No social circle. No emergency contacts. No family on file. Rarely left their units."

Mara didn't argue. That was its own answer.

My hands were still on the edge of her desk, but I could feel the way my body had changed—like my muscles had decided I was on duty again.

These weren't random people.

These were people who lived alone.

With no friends or relatives.

I let the silence sit between us for a beat, forcing Mara to live in it with me.

Then I asked the question that I already knew would turn the room.

"Did they pay their rent on time?"

Mara's relief returned, thin and quick. *Procedure. I can answer procedure.*

"Yes," she said. "None of them had any problems paying because most or all of their rent was funded by AESS."

My jaw tightened because I already knew the answer to the next question.

"Did the rent continue after they disappeared?"

Mara's eyes darted to the hallway and back. Not paranoia. Not guilt. Reflex.

"Yes," she said.

Yes.

The word didn't belong in a world where missing people were supposed to trigger alarms. It belonged to a system designed to keep money flowing, no matter who vanished inside it. A world I had seen from above, from my seat in the AG's office. And now I'd been introduced to it from the inside, where it was actually happening.

"Did you notify the Westbridges that the tenants were missing?"

Mara hesitated, then nodded.

"Yes," she said quietly. "Gareth told me to."

"Did you do it in writing?"

She shook her head quickly, as if the idea itself were dangerous. "No. Gareth told me to never put anything like that in writing. I was always supposed to call."

I felt the room shift. Not physically—emotionally. Like the office had become smaller, like the air had thickened.

I forced my brain to stay in step. One question at a time. Control.

"How long after they disappeared did the rent keep coming?" I asked.

Mara's fingers tapped lightly against the paper as she did the math she'd done before. "About three months."

Three months.

Long enough for a human story to cool.

Long enough for neighbors to stop asking.

Long enough for an office to move on.

Long enough for money to be redirected without anyone noticing—unless someone had already been trained to see patterns instead of incidents.

I stared at the open folder, but I wasn't seeing it anymore. I was seeing transaction summaries. Funnel accounts. The convergence.

North Meridian.

My call to the feds.

My firing.

The severance folder squared to the edge of a desk like symmetry could make betrayal clean.

Mara shifted in her chair, misreading my silence as hesitation. "Kate—"

I looked up. "Tell me about Gareth Cole," I said.

Mara's shoulders tightened as if the name had weight.

"The Super before you," she said. "Apartment 601. Sixth floor. End of the hall."

A detail that mattered more than it should have. End of the hall meant fewer neighbors. Fewer eyes. A quieter disappearance.

"When did he go missing?"

"Just after Christmas. So, about a month ago."

A month.

Long enough for panic to fade. Long enough for routines to reset. Long enough for someone important to decide how the story would be told.

"And the police?" I asked.

Mara frowned, her voice dropping. "There was no report."

That landed harder than anything else she'd said.

The Westbridges hadn't waited for him to be found. They hadn't treated it like a crisis. They'd simply started looking for his replacement.

Like a position had opened.

Not that a person had vanished.

"What was he like?" I asked.

Mara stared at the file in front of her as if it might accuse her. "Quiet," she said. "Did his job. Didn't cause waves. Didn't... socialize much. No family on file that I know of. He lived alone."

"And he ordered the units sealed," I said.

Mara nodded once, small and reluctant. "He told Ray and me not to touch certain doors. Not to clear them. Not to re-rent them."

Not to re-rent them.

Containment, not management.

The phrase from yesterday came back with a chill:

*That wasn't property management. That was absolute control.*

I sat back slowly, and the chair creaked under me—an ordinary sound that felt too loud.

A thought slid in, unwanted but undeniable, and it didn't come from paranoia. It came from math.

My father was gone. Left when I was nine and never came back.

My mother passed away three years ago.

My sister was estranged. Living in Maine, last I heard.

No spouse. No kids. No boyfriend.

No one who would file a missing-person report with urgency.

No one who would kick down doors to find me.

No one who would make noise.

I'd always told myself I was the hunter. The investigator. The person who walked into systems and forced them to explain themselves.

But the pattern didn't care about my job title.

The pattern cared about isolation.

And isolation was the one thing my life had in abundance.

I looked at the tenant files again—Keene, Rosen, Morales—three names on paper, three apartments with the tenants removed like organs cut out of a living body.

I shuffled through Gareth Cole's file, not really seeing anything, just processing all that I'd learned. It was a lot to take in.

Then I heard my own thoughts with a clarity that made my stomach turn.

I fit.

I wasn't the hunter.

I was the kind of prey this building consumed.

And the worst part was how quickly the realization settled into place—as if some part of me had known it the moment Mark Westbridge said, *rent-free*, and smiled like a man handing you a life raft without telling you it leaked.

I'd been an investigator for a long time. Had good instincts. And while that part of my brain was screaming, *Run!!!*, another part, deeper inside me, was saying, *Keep going. You're strong enough to survive this.*

I just had to figure out which one of me was right.

# CHAPTER 13

THE REVIEW OF the missing people with Mara had changed everything.

I didn't have all the answers yet—but I had a shape. A pattern. A theory that fit too well to ignore.

If it was right, I was standing inside something much larger than a handful of missing tenants.

I needed proof before I did anything stupid.

So I asked the next question.

"Is there a master key that opens every apartment?"

"Why do you want to know that?" she asked.

I almost laughed.

People only asked that when the answer was dangerous.

"Mara, how much do the Westbridges pay you?"

Her eyes flicked to the door, then back to me.

"What's that got to do with anything?" she asked.

I smiled, just enough to keep it friendly. Just enough to keep her talking.

"Mara, how much are you paid to work here?"

The question had landed wrong. I could see it in her face. This wasn't in any script she'd memorized.

"That's... not really—"

"I'm not asking out of curiosity," I said gently. "I'm trying to understand how this place works."

She hesitated. Then, almost reluctantly, she said it.

"Ninety-eight thousand."

The number slid between us like something fragile.

I kept my expression neutral, but inside, everything rearranged.

Ninety-eight thousand dollars.

More than most building managers made.

More than I made—unless you counted the free luxury apartment.

Mara lived off-site. Paid her own rent, presumably. But she made enough to live well in this town.

For clerical work.

For filing leases.

For answering phones.

For knowing which apartments were sealed and which people had disappeared. And staying quiet about it.

That wasn't a salary.

That was a payoff.

Mara watched my face carefully, like she was bracing for something to break.

"You don't have to tell me why," I said quietly. "I already know."

She swallowed.

And suddenly her fear made perfect sense.

"Okay," I said. "No worries. So, is there a master key that opens every apartment?"

"Yes," she said. "Of course there is."

"Does it open the penthouse units too?"

She hesitated—just a fraction of a second—but it was enough.

"Yes."

The room shifted, just slightly.

"How many master keys are there?" I asked.

Mara folded her hands on the desk, as if arranging something she wanted to keep from sliding apart.

"There are three," she said. "One stays here in the office. One is with Ray. And one is over at Westbridge."

I nodded slowly, like this was just another administrative detail.

But inside, the implications were snapping into place.

Three keys.

Three points of access.

Three ways in and out of any apartment in this building—mine included.

The missing tenants hadn't vanished from sealed rooms.

They had vanished from controlled ones.

So had Gareth.

And so could I.

I didn't let any of that reach my face. Mara was still watching me, measuring my reaction, the way people do when they're afraid they've just said too much.

"Where's the master key here in the office kept?" I asked.

She gestured to a locked drawer beneath her desk. "In there. We hardly ever use it."

"Good," I said. "I'll hold onto it for now. Please get it for me."

Mara froze.

Just for a second.

And that was when I knew I was already inside the machinery of whatever this place was hiding—and it was far bigger than a few missing people and a crooked rent trail.

Then she unlocked the drawer.

I took the key and closed my hand around it.

Calm on the surface.

Already planning.

I closed the Penthouse door behind me and stood still, listening.

The place was too quiet. Not the comfortable quiet of an empty room, but the kind that felt recently occupied, as if the air itself hadn't yet decided whether it was safe to relax. I'd learned a long time ago that silence was only neutral when it was honest.

This silence wasn't.

The locksmith wasn't due for another forty minutes. That gave me time to do what I always did when I entered a new space that might not actually be mine.

I set my bag on the kitchen counter and took out the scanner.

It was small—about the size of a paperback—but tuned to pick up low-power RF emissions, the kind used by listening devices and cameras, cheap or expensive. I moved slowly, deliberately, letting it sweep the room in narrow arcs the way I used to walk a crime scene.

The first hit came almost immediately.

The scanner chirped softly beneath the kitchen cabinets. I crouched, tracking the signal until I found it—a pinhead-sized black lens tucked into the shadow behind the range hood. Whoever put it there hadn't even tried to hide it well. They hadn't needed to.

I popped it loose with a butter knife and sealed it in a zippered evidence pouch.

One.

The living room took longer. I checked the lamps, the baseboards, the television, the art on the walls. The scanner stayed quiet until I passed the built-in bookshelf by the window. There, hidden beside a row of decorative hardcovers no one had ever read, was another tiny camera pointed straight at the couch.

Two.

The bedroom was last.

I slowed when I crossed the threshold. Being watched where you slept was different. The scanner didn't chirp at first—but when it did, the signal was stronger.

The device was hidden behind the headboard, angled down toward the bed.

Three.

I removed it and sealed it with the others.

Three rooms. Three bugs. No hesitation. No testing phase.

They hadn't been placed by someone guessing. They'd been installed by someone who had keys.

I stood in the middle of the bedroom for a moment, holding the pouch.

So this was what rent-free meant.

I slid the pouch into my bag and turned to the next problem.

The router.

The one that had been waiting for me sat on a console table in the living room, blinking softly, broadcasting its friendly blue light. I unplugged it and set it aside.

Then I opened the box I'd brought back from the store.

It wasn't something you bought at a big-box electronics chain. I'd driven across town to a networking supply shop that catered to businesses and paranoid IT professionals. The clerk hadn't even blinked when I asked for something that couldn't be remotely administered, couldn't be mirrored, and wouldn't accept firmware updates without physical authorization.

I'd bought two.

I set the first one up on the kitchen counter and quickly configured it. Within minutes, the Penthouse was running on a private, encrypted network that only I controlled.

Whoever had been listening before was now deaf.

I let myself take one slow breath.

The doorbell rang.

I checked the peephole before opening it. The locksmith stood in the hall, tool case in hand, already studying the frame.

He worked efficiently. The old lock came out too easily, which told me more than I wanted about how often it had been opened with something other than a key. The new one went in solid and heavy, reinforced with a deadbolt that looked more suited to a safe than an apartment.

When he finished, the door locked with a new sound—a deeper, final click that made my shoulders loosen just a fraction.

Physical security. Digital security.

A perimeter.

After he left, I did one more slow sweep of the apartment. The scanner stayed quiet.

Good.

I glanced at the second router still in its unopened box.

That one was for later.

For now, the penthouse was clean.

I went to the window and looked out over Phoenix, the city glowing in the afternoon heat, unaware that a quiet war had just started several stories above it.

They wanted to spy on me in my home.

They'd have to do better than this.

The lobby was empty when I came back downstairs.

Not the friendly kind of empty. The late-night kind—where every sound feels amplified, and every corner feels like it might be holding something you're not supposed to see. The overhead lights had been dimmed to evening mode, throwing long reflections across the polished tile floor. The elevator chimed somewhere above me and then went silent.

Mara was gone for the day.

I needed her gone because, based on what I had learned from her earlier in the day, there was a strong possibility that anything I said or did while Mara was present would find its way back to the Westbridges.

Their glass-and-stone office in the Camelback Corridor was where the real control sat.

This place was just a relay.

I let myself into the office with my new key and closed the door behind me.

The air smelled faintly of toner and carpet cleaner — sterile, institutional. The kind of smell that told you people had been here earlier, doing ordinary things, filing leases, answering phones, scheduling repairs. The kind of smell that made it easier to forget what else happened here when the doors were shut.

I dropped my bag on the empty chair across from Mara's desk and took out the scanner.

Small. Handheld. The kind private investigators used when they didn't want to trust a room.

I started where Mara sat every day.

The scanner chirped softly as I passed it over the desktop. Over the phone. Over the keyboard. Over the blotter where she kept handwritten notes.

Nothing.

Then I swept the edge of the monitor.

A sharp spike lit the screen.

I leaned closer, angling the scanner until it locked onto the source — a tiny black dot no bigger than a grain of rice, tucked just beneath the lip of the display.

A microphone.

Of course it was.

Mara didn't need to be wired.

Her desk already was.

I slid a thin blade from my pocket and popped the casing loose. The mic came free with a soft click. I dropped it into a small evidence bag and wrote on the label without thinking:

Office — Front Desk

Then I moved on.

The phone base.

The power strip.

The underside of the desk.

Clean.

Which meant whoever planted that first bug knew exactly where Mara spent her time.

I crossed into the back office — the one that was supposed to be mine now.

The door shut with a quiet finality behind me.

This room had been Gareth Cole's once. The missing Super's. The place where sealed doors had been ordered, where units had been labeled "don't touch," where decisions had been made that didn't make sense unless you were part of the conspiracy or afraid of the ones who were. I didn't know which group Gareth Cole belonged to, but I did know that someone wasn't happy about what he'd been doing, and he was gone.

I swept the scanner slowly over the desk.

Nothing.

The file cabinet.

Nothing.

The wall by the light switch.

A faint pulse.

I leaned closer and found it — another mic, taped

behind the plastic plate, wired into the wall like it had always belonged there.

Listening.

Recording.

Feeding something that wasn't in this building.

I removed it and bagged it too.

Office — Back Room

Two bugs. Two desks. Two points of control.

Mara might not have known she was being monitored.

Or she might have known and learned how to live with it.

Either way, everything that happened in this office was being relayed somewhere else.

I set the scanner aside and took out the second router I'd bought earlier — the one I hadn't told Mara about.

Just like the other one, it wasn't fancy. It wasn't sleek. It was functional and secure, designed for small offices that didn't want to be hacked.

I unplugged the existing router — the one the building had installed — and set it on the floor.

Then I connected mine.

By the time I finished, the office was running on a network the Westbridges didn't control.

Tomorrow, I would give Mara the new login and tell her it was just an upgrade.

She would report it.

I didn't care.

Let them know the pipe had changed.

Let them wonder what else had.

I zipped my bag and headed for the door.

That was when I saw him.

Evan Pike stood just outside the office, leaning against the wall like he'd been there for a while.

Waiting.

"Working late?" he asked.

His voice was casual. Too casual. His eyes moved — not to my face, but to my bag.

To what I was carrying.

"Something like that," I said.

He didn't move aside.

"You're not supposed to be in there after hours," he said.

"I'm the Super," I replied. "That means I'm supposed to be anywhere I want to be."

His mouth twitched. Not quite a smile.

"Yeah," he said. "That's what Gareth used to say."

My pulse jumped.

"Gareth didn't understand what he was standing in," I said. "I do."

For a moment, something unreadable passed through his eyes.

Then he stepped back.

I walked past him without breaking stride.

Behind me, he said quietly, "Be careful who you listen to in this place."

I didn't turn around. He wasn't worth the confirmation.

# CHAPTER 14

I ARRIVED AT THE Ashford the next morning with one large suitcase and every intention of making the place functional, if not comfortable. I still had a month left on the lease at my old apartment, which meant I didn't have to pretend this was home yet.

The encounter with Evan Pike still lived in my body. Not as fear—fear burned hot and then faded—but as awareness. The kind that sharpened your senses and refused to let you relax. He hadn't threatened me. He hadn't needed to. He had simply reminded me that Gareth Cole had once stood where I was standing now, and that this building had already swallowed one Super whole.

I let myself into the private elevator and rode it up alone. No music. No floor numbers. Just the quiet rise through a building that suddenly felt less like a place to live and more like a vertical maze.

When the doors opened onto the penthouse floor, nothing had changed from the night before—but it felt different. The thick carpet. The warm lighting. The silence that was too complete. It all read now as controlled rather than luxurious.

I unlocked the door and stepped inside.

The apartment was still staged, still impersonal. Nothing about it reflected a life. No mail on the counter. No shoes by the door. No half-empty coffee cups. It was a space designed to look occupied without ever actually being lived in.

I closed the door behind me and set my suitcase down just inside the entryway.

This was not home.

This was a forward operating base.

I shrugged off my blazer and hung it in the closet, then knelt and unzipped the suitcase. I had packed efficiently—clothes rolled tight, toiletries in sealed bags, shoes tucked into the corners. Everything I would need for the next month, maybe longer, while I decided whether this place was something I could survive inside.

The first thing I took out wasn't a sweater or a toothbrush.

It was my Glock 19.

I hadn't carried a weapon since I left the Phoenix Police Department. Even during the months after the AG's office cut me loose—when my life was unstable and my future uncertain—I hadn't felt the need. But that was before I'd learned how many people had vanished inside this building, and before a man with too-watchful eyes had reminded me that Gareth Cole once thought he was in control, too.

I kept my shooting skills current at the Scottsdale

Gun Club. Muscle memory doesn't fade. Neither does instinct.

I threaded the holster onto my belt and settled the weight of the gun against my hip. It felt heavy—but reassuring. When I put the blazer back on later, it would disappear just enough to keep it hidden from anyone who wasn't looking for it. And for those who were looking, I was protected by Arizona's open-carry law. I hadn't needed to exercise this right in quite a while, but circumstances had changed for me.

And not for the better.

I stood for a moment in the quiet penthouse, breathing in air that smelled faintly of expensive cleaning solution and nothing else.

Too big.

Too quiet.

I moved through the rooms, opening doors, familiarizing myself with the layout as if I were clearing a space rather than inhabiting it. The bedroom was vast and unused. The kitchen was pristine. The living room felt more like a hotel lobby than a place someone would actually sit down and relax.

Then I walked into the gym.

It wasn't a spare room with a treadmill shoved into a corner. It was a full conversion — a former bedroom stripped down and rebuilt around my habits. A rowing machine, resistance stations, a treadmill, the same equipment I'd used for years at my old gym uptown.

They hadn't guessed.

They had known.

Good.

I would need it.

After unpacking my clothes into the closet and placing my toiletries in the bathroom, I zipped the empty suitcase shut and pushed it under the bed. This place might never feel like home, but it needed to function like one if I was going to survive here.

I slipped the blazer back on, feeling the weight of the Glock settle invisibly against my side, and headed for the door.

The first visit of the day waited below.

And for the first time since I'd taken this job, I understood exactly what I was walking into.

I took the service elevator down.

It was the only way to reach the residential floors from the penthouse without stepping back into the lobby, and I wasn't in the mood to be seen. The private elevator was fast and discreet—but it only ran between the ground floor and the top. Anything else meant going through the building the way everyone else did.

I preferred the back routes. They were quieter. And they didn't leave witnesses.

The hallway on the fourth floor smelled faintly of carpet cleaner and something stale beneath it. Apartment 411 sat three doors from the stairwell, a beige door with a brushed-metal handle and no distinguishing marks. No wreath. No welcome mat. No sign that anyone inside had ever expected a visitor.

I slid the master key into the lock.

The click was too loud.

It shouldn't have been — it was just a mechanical

sound — but it rang in my ears anyway. A boundary crossed. A line stepped over.

I reminded myself that I was the Super. That this was my job.

It didn't make it feel any less like breaking in.

The door swung inward.

Keene's apartment was dim, the blinds half-closed, the air heavy with the smell of something that had been sealed too long. Stale coffee. Dust. The faint, dry trace of fabric that hadn't moved in months.

It was still a home.

A jacket hung on the back of a chair. A pair of sneakers sat beside the couch. A half-read paperback lay face down on the coffee table, a crease breaking its spine like someone had set it down intending to come back.

Mail was stacked on the small entry table — not scattered, not trashed. Neatly piled. Utility bills. Circulars. Two envelopes from a bank I recognized.

Eight months of a life quietly waiting.

I closed the door behind me and locked it, more out of instinct than necessity. If someone came down this hallway, I wanted to hear them before seeing them.

I moved slowly, methodically, the way I had in hundreds of apartments and offices and houses over the years. No rushing. No assumptions. Just letting my eyes tell me what didn't belong.

The kitchen was clean but lived in. A mug in the sink. Dishes in the drying rack. Nothing that suggested someone had packed up and left.

The bedroom was the same. Clothes hung in the closet in an ordinary, boring gradient of work shirts and jeans.

Shoes lined up below. A suitcase leaned against the back wall, empty.

He hadn't been preparing to go anywhere.

I checked drawers. Nightstand. Bathroom cabinet. Still nothing that felt like an answer. Just a man who had gone to bed one night and never come back.

So I narrowed my focus.

I wasn't here for closure.

I was here for access.

I went to the small desk in the corner of the living room. A basic setup — laptop stand, a few cables, a stack of unopened mail. Beneath it sat a slim file box. I pulled it out and opened it.

Bingo.

Bank statements. Insurance. A few tax documents. Everything a person who didn't trust the cloud would keep close.

I flipped through carefully, not tearing, not disturbing more than I had to. Most of it was routine — checking accounts, a modest savings balance, nothing flashy.

Then I found the checkbook.

It was tucked into a leather sleeve, the kind with pockets inside the front and back covers. People used them to hold registers, deposit slips... and sometimes things they didn't want to lose.

I slid a finger inside the back flap.

There was a folded piece of paper.

Not hidden, exactly — just placed somewhere no one ever thought to look.

I unfolded it.

A username.

A password.

Just what I needed.

I didn't smile.

I didn't react at all.

I just folded the paper back exactly the way I had found it and slid it into my pocket.

Keene's apartment was still quiet behind me, still waiting for a man who wasn't coming back.

I left everything else as it was.

Some doors, once opened, don't need to be forced any wider.

The hallway on the third floor felt different.

Not in any way you could point to on a floor plan — same carpet, same beige doors, same recessed lights humming faintly overhead — but the air was heavier here. As if the building itself had learned to keep its voice down.

Apartment 318 sat between two occupied units. A plant with browned leaves leaned against one neighbor's doorframe. From the other side came the muted sound of a television. Life continuing.

I slid the master key into the lock.

This one didn't resist the way Keene's had. The door opened easily, almost too easily, as if it had been waiting.

Inside, the apartment was small and dim, the blinds drawn almost completely shut. A single lamp glowed near the couch, casting soft light across a space that felt more fragile than abandoned.

Again, this wasn't a place someone had walked away from.

This was a place someone had been living inside carefully.

A knitted throw lay folded on the arm of the couch. A pair of slippers sat side by side near the coffee table. On the wall, framed photos showed a woman with thinning hair smiling beside different nurses, different hospital rooms, different seasons passing.

Lila Rosen.

Her presence was everywhere — not loud, not dramatic, just quietly persistent.

I closed the door behind me.

The smell of antiseptic lingered faintly beneath the normal scent of an apartment. Clean, but in a way that came from trying too hard to keep illness at bay.

I moved slowly, the way I had in Keene's place, but my steps felt more intrusive here. He had been organized. Contained.

She had been... surviving.

On the small kitchen counter sat pill bottles lined up like sentries. Names. Dosages. Instructions. A printed medication schedule lay beside them, neatly highlighted.

She hadn't been preparing to leave.

She'd been preparing to make it through the week.

A thin stack of envelopes sat on the table — hospital bills, insurance correspondence, government letters stamped with barcodes and official warnings. I didn't read them closely, but I didn't need to.

This apartment wasn't a home. It was a safety net stretched just tight enough to keep someone from falling.

I checked the bedroom next. The bed was made with

care, corners tucked tight. A heating pad lay folded at the foot, ready for use. A walker rested beside the dresser.

Lila Rosen wasn't someone who disappeared on impulse.

I went through drawers and folders, gently, returning things to where they belonged. Medical files. A few hundred dollars in cash tucked inside a book. A debit card taped to a folded piece of paper with an emergency number written in shaky ink.

But no account logins.

No passwords.

No folded slips hidden inside checkbook sleeves.

What I did find was a desktop computer on a small desk in the corner of the living room — older, dusty, still plugged in. The screen was dark.

I made a mental note.

This wasn't a dead end.

It was just unfinished business. I could return later if I needed to.

I stood in the middle of Lila Rosen's apartment and let the weight of it settle.

Keene's place had felt like someone paused mid-sentence.

This felt like someone had been silenced.

I locked the door behind me when I left, the click echoing softly in the quiet hallway.

One apartment had given me what I was looking for.

The other had given me a reason not to stop.

The door to 506 opened onto yet another tragic scene.

Not abandoned.

Interrupted.

The air inside was warmer than the other units, faintly scented with food and detergent and something human that hadn't had time to fade yet. Shoes were lined up neatly by the door—work boots, running shoes, a pair of worn sneakers. A jacket hung on the back of a chair, one sleeve still half-turned inside out like he'd taken it off in a hurry.

I closed the door quietly behind me.

The kitchen was small but lived in. A half-empty carton of milk in the fridge. Leftover takeout in plastic containers. A loaf of moldy bread on the counter. The clock on the microwave still blinking twelve-oh-oh, like no one had been here to reset it.

This wasn't the home of someone who'd decided to leave.

This was the home of someone who expected to come back.

I moved slowly, deliberately, letting my eyes absorb the room before I touched anything. A single plate drying on the rack. A mug in the sink with a ring of coffee at the bottom. A grocery receipt folded neatly beside a set of keys.

And then I saw it.

A folded piece of paper pinned to the refrigerator with a small magnet.

Not hidden.

Not tucked into a drawer.

Right where he'd see it every day.

I slid it free.

Account numbers.

Usernames.

A handwritten password.

Three security-question answers written in careful block letters.

Full banking access.

It didn't matter that it was out in the open.

No one ever came in here but him.

People who have visitors hide things.

People who live alone don't bother.

That was the point.

I exhaled slowly, the shape of the trap coming into focus in my mind.

This was the live wire.

Javier Morales wasn't just missing — he was still being used. I would bet that his account was still active. Still paying rent. Still quietly feeding the system that had erased him.

Whoever was doing it would have to come back here, digitally, to change the flow of money.

And when they did...

I would be ready.

# CHAPTER 15

I LEFT THE ASHFORD late in the morning, riding the private elevator down alone.

Being alone didn't calm me. Not in this place.

In this place, privacy meant fewer witnesses.

The lobby was quiet. A few tenants passing through. A courier wheeling a cart toward the elevators. Normal, unremarkable movement—the kind that made it easier for someone to disappear inside it.

I stepped outside into the bright January sun and walked two blocks before I flagged a taxi. I could have driven, but if someone was following me, I didn't want to make it easy for them.

We passed by a big-box electronics store where I could have bought what I needed. But it would have meant cameras, receipts, loyalty programs, and databases designed to remember you.

I chose a gas station instead.

One of the bigger ones on a busy corner, with a convenience store attached and a dozen people cycling in and out. Lottery tickets. Cigarettes. Soda. Nobody paying attention to anyone else.

I picked up a prepaid smartphone from a rack near the register.

No contract. No name. No address.

I paid in cash.

The clerk didn't look up.

Outside, I peeled the plastic from the box and dropped it in a trash can already overflowing with coffee cups and scratch-off tickets. The phone fit easily into my coat pocket. Light. Unassuming. A device designed for one thing—anonymity.

Back at The Ashford, I rode the private elevator up to the penthouse.

The doors slid open to quiet. Thick carpet. Filtered light. A space so insulated from the city it felt unreal, like a luxury bunker built above the noise.

I set the burner phone on the kitchen counter.

Then I opened my laptop and connected to my own router—the one I had installed the day before. My network. My airspace. Not the building's. Not the office's. Not anyone else's.

I created a new email account.

Fake name.

Fake birthday.

Fake recovery questions.

I wrote the password down once, then memorized it and destroyed the scrap of paper.

The burner chimed as I powered it on.

No contacts.

No history.

No trail.

Yet.

I stared at the phone for a moment longer than necessary.

Once I used this number to touch a financial system, it would be inside the crime whether I liked it or not.

There was no clean way to do what came next.

Only a careful one.

I went to the website of Thomas Keene's bank.

And logged into his account.

The page loaded.

No spinning wheel. No error message. No security challenge.

Just a dashboard.

Thomas Keene's name in the upper corner.

A balance.

A list of transactions.

Which meant something important all by itself.

He hadn't enabled secondary security.

No text codes.

No app approvals.

No one-time passwords.

For a man who lived quietly, worked remotely, and kept to himself, it made a bleak kind of sense. If no one ever came into your apartment, if no one ever touched your things, why would you imagine anyone trying to get inside your bank account?

I didn't let myself linger on the ethics of what I was doing.

That debate was over the moment I'd stepped into 411.

I clicked into Payments & Transfers.

Then Automatic Payments.

There it was.

A line item that had once looked as ordinary as gravity.

Westbridge Property Management.

Monthly rent.

Routing number.

Account number.

Scheduled.

Except it wasn't active anymore.

It had been turned off.

Not missed.

Not late.

Not disputed.

Canceled.

I clicked into the history.

The last payment to Westbridge had gone out five months ago—three months after Thomas Keene vanished.

Below it was a new line.

A corporate account at North Meridian Private Bank.

A bank I remembered well from my last days at the AG.

Everything about the electronic fund transfer was the same as the Westbridge payment, except for the destination.

Same amount.

Same timing.

Same frequency.

Only the destination had changed.

Now it was a corporate account at North Meridian

Private Bank. One of three, as I remembered. And all three of them were routing the funds to a foundation in Luxembourg.

I opened the transaction details.

There were the routing numbers.

The account identifiers.

The reference codes.

The digital fingerprints of a system doing exactly what it had been designed to do.

This wasn't theory.

This wasn't pattern recognition.

This was money moving, month after month, out of an account belonging to a man who no longer existed in any meaningful way... into the same private bank I had found to be receiving public assistance funds in my old job.

North Meridian.

Inside my building.

Inside my new job.

I scrolled backward.

Each payment was annotated with a bland internal memo.

Rent — Unit 411

As if Thomas Keene were still there.

As if someone were still unlocking the door.

As if a life hadn't simply stopped one day and been replaced by a financial institution.

I sat back slowly.

Eight months of payments.

Eight months of silence.

Eight months of a man being gone while his money kept reporting for duty.

And someone—somewhere—had told the system exactly when to make that switch.

Not the building.

Not Westbridge Property Management. I didn't believe they had done it. Yes, they were complicit, because they knew the tenant was missing and didn't report it to AESS. But they didn't do it. They hired me to find who did. They just hadn't told me that yet.

It was someone else.

Someone who knew when Thomas Keene disappeared.

Someone who knew when to redirect the money.

Someone who had access to his banking infrastructure.

I closed the tab without logging out.

Not yet.

One confirmation was enough to turn suspicion into certainty.

And now I knew something else.

For sure.

Javier Morales's account contained the bait I would set to catch them.

I logged into Javier Morales's account.

Anyone careless enough to leave his credentials on his fridge wasn't going to bother with secondary security.

He hadn't.

I was in.

The dashboard loaded with a soft, harmless chime that felt grotesquely out of place. Blue and white panels. Clean lines. A reassuring interface designed to make people feel safe while their lives were quietly being rearranged.

Checking. Savings. Linked payments.

Javier Morales had never been wealthy, but he hadn't been desperate either. A steady warehouse job through a temp agency. Modest deposits. Including the monthly subsidy from AESS. Rent paid like clockwork.

And there it was.

An automatic payment.

Still active.

Still flowing.

To Westbridge Property Management.

I sat back slightly, letting out a breath I hadn't realized I'd been holding. This was the only account that still mattered. Thomas Keene's and Lila Rosen's AESS deposits had already been rerouted. Their money had been harvested and redirected.

Javier's was the live wire, because he'd been gone for just under three months.

This was the one they would have to come back for. And they'd be coming soon.

At the three-month mark, just days from now, whoever was pulling the strings would log into his account and redirect the funds to North Meridian Private Bank.

I didn't touch anything yet.

Not a single setting.

Not a single checkbox.

That was the mistake amateurs made—changing things too soon, tipping their hand.

What I did instead was set up the quietest thing possible.

Alerts.

Every login.

Every failed attempt.

Every device.

Every location.

Every change.

And I routed them to a number and an email address that didn't exist yesterday.

The burner phone sat on the counter beside me, dark and silent, waiting for the first ghost to tap on the glass.

No alarms.

No flags.

No warnings sent back to the user.

Just a whisper when someone entered the room.

I saved the settings.

Closed the window.

Logged out.

Javier Morales's account was no longer just a victim.

It was bait.

And now I had everything I needed.

One account that proved where the money went.

And one that would tell me who touched it.

If I lived long enough for them to come calling.

# CHAPTER 16

THAT AFTERNOON, I went down to the office and tried to act like a superintendent rather than an investigator.

I wasn't sure how much the Westbridges actually cared about the superintendent role—Mara and Ray already kept the building running the way they wanted it to—but I needed to understand how the place worked day to day.

The routines.

The rhythms.

The moments when people walked in with small problems and didn't know there was something much bigger going on in the place they called home.

Mara sat at her desk in the main office, headset on, fingers moving with practiced efficiency across the keyboard. Lease forms. Maintenance tickets. Rent notices. The machinery of ordinary life.

I left my office door open on purpose.

It let me hear everything.

And it let everyone see me.

A superintendent who hid behind a closed door was a superintendent who didn't want to be disturbed. I wanted to be disturbed. I wanted to be part of the building's daily noise, the small annoyances and casual confessions that people only shared when they believed nothing important was happening.

The first tenant came in five minutes later.

He was middle-aged, nervous, holding a folded piece of paper. His complaint was about a ceiling fan that rattled at night. Mara nodded sympathetically, logged the ticket, promised maintenance would look at it.

He left relieved.

The building took another quiet breath.

Next came a woman asking about a package that hadn't arrived. Then a man who thought his neighbor was smoking marijuana on the balcony. Mara handled them all with polite calm. I listened from behind my desk, pretending to sort paperwork while my attention cataloged voices, timing, who lingered, who rushed.

This was how patterns began.

Not with crime scenes.

With inconvenience.

Ray hadn't come by yet. I noticed that too.

He usually made a loop through the office once every afternoon. To pick up parts. To update Mara on what he'd been up to that morning, to lean against her desk and complain about elevators.

Today, he was late.

I told myself not to read too much into that.

This wasn't about Ray.

Not yet.

I made a few notes in a blank notebook—who had come in, what they'd said, how Mara had responded. Routine established the baseline. Anything that broke it would stand out later.

It struck me as ironic that the role of a superintendent wasn't all that different from the core work of an investigator.

Understanding what normal looked like.

So you could recognize when it wasn't.

And that was when the door opened again.

Mrs. Lien Tran came in carrying a folded utility bill and an apologetic smile.

She was small, neatly dressed, hair pulled back with the kind of care that suggested habit rather than vanity. She waited until Mara looked up before speaking, as if she didn't want to interrupt whatever important business was happening behind the desk.

"Excuse me," she said softly. "I'm sorry to bother you. My kitchen light keeps flickering. I tried changing the bulb, but it still does it."

Mara turned in her chair, already reaching for a form. "That's not a problem at all," she said. "Let me get that logged. Which apartment?"

"Four-ten," Mrs. Tran said.

I was sitting in my office with the door open, pretending to read a maintenance report. The number made my eyes flick up.

410.

While Mara typed, I slid my mouse across the desk and pulled up the resident database. Lien Tran appeared on the screen.

Apartment 410.

Directly across the hall from Thomas Keene's 411.

My pulse stayed steady, but my attention sharpened. This was an opportunity.

Mara finished filling out the ticket. "I'll have maintenance come by this afternoon," she said. "You don't need to be home if you don't want to be."

Mrs. Tran nodded gratefully. "Thank you. I appreciate it."

That was my cue.

I stood and stepped out of my office into the main room. "Mrs. Tran?" I said.

She turned, surprised but pleased.

"I'm Kate," I said. "The new superintendent."

Her face lit up. "Oh. Hello."

"Mara's going to take care of your light," I said. "But would you mind stepping into my office for a moment? I just have a couple of questions."

She looked instinctively to Mara.

Mara nodded. "It's fine," she said. "Go ahead."

Mrs. Tran followed me with a little flutter of curiosity, like she'd been invited somewhere important.

I closed the door behind us, gently.

"Please," I said, gesturing to the chair. "Have a seat."

She perched on the edge of it, smoothing her skirt.

"You've lived here a while, haven't you?" I asked.

"Six years," she said proudly.

"That's a long time," I said. "You must know the building very well."

She smiled. "I do."

I let a beat pass before continuing.

"I was just looking at the resident list," I said casually. "I see you're right across the hall from Thomas Keene."

Her smile faded.

Just a little. But enough.

"Yes," she said. "He was very quiet."

"When was the last time you saw him?" I asked.

She thought. "It was a long time ago. Let's see. That apartment has been empty since last April. So, probably eight or nine months ago. Do you know why they haven't rented it out yet?"

"No, I'm sorry Mrs. Tran. I don't know. I'm new. Just trying to get the lay of land at this point."

"I understand," she said.

"If you think back to when Mr. Keene was still around, did you notice anything unusual around that time? Anyone coming or going who seemed out of place?"

Her first answer came quickly.

"Evan Pike," she said. "But he's always around. He walks everywhere."

I nodded, like that matched what I already knew.

Then she hesitated.

Her fingers tightened around the folded bill in her lap.

"And... Ray," she said.

"Ray from maintenance?" I asked.

She nodded. "Yes. I saw him go into Thomas's apartment."

"Before or after Thomas stopped coming home?" I asked.

"Both," she said.

The word settled between us.

"Why do you think he was there before?" I asked gently.

"I assumed it was just maintenance," she said. "Ray is always fixing things."

"Did you ever ask Mr. Keene about it?" I asked.

She shook her head slowly.

"I didn't get the chance," she said. "I never saw Thomas again after that."

Silence filled the small office. The picture shifted. *What were you doing in there, Ray?*

"Thank you," I said finally. "That was very helpful."

She looked relieved. "I'm glad I could help."

I walked her back to the main office. She thanked Mara again and left, carrying her flickering-light problem back out into the afternoon.

I went back into my office and sat, thinking.

Ray had been inside Thomas Keene's apartment before he vanished.

And after.

Could Ray be the key to all of this? Maybe. Maybe not. I'd definitely speak to him, and as it turned out, he wanted to speak to me too.

Ray arrived within minutes of Mrs. Tran leaving.

Mara was still finishing up the work order when he stepped into the office, his presence filling the doorway—not loud, not rushed, just there. A man who knew every inch of the building didn't need to hurry.

"Flickering light in 410," Mara said. "Mrs. Tran."

Ray nodded. "I'll take care of it."

Then he paused.

"Before I do," he added, glancing toward my office, "I just need a minute with Kate."

Mara looked up, mildly surprised, but she didn't object.

"Okay," she said.

I could see her eyes from across the room. Even from here, I could tell it was a warning.

She was telling him with her eyes to be careful.

Ray gave a small nod and turned toward my office.

He stepped inside and closed the door behind him—not sharply, not to make a point. Just enough to keep the conversation from carrying. He remained standing.

"I water the plants in your penthouse once a week," he said. "Part of my rounds."

I didn't interrupt.

"I tried to get in earlier," he went on. "My key didn't work. I just wanted to make sure everything was okay."

That was the part that landed.

Not that he'd tried.

That he'd noticed so quickly.

"I changed the locks," I said evenly.

Ray blinked—genuine surprise flickering across his face.

"You could've asked me to do that."

I let the silence sit for half a beat.

"I didn't realize you handled that kind of thing," I said. "It's done now, though. I can take care of the plants myself."

A boundary. Calmly placed.

Ray studied me—not irritated, not offended—just recalibrating.

"Okay," he said.

I shifted slightly in my chair, as if something had just occurred to me.

"Since I've got you here, can I ask you something?"

He nodded.

"Thomas Keene," I said. "Apartment 411."

His face didn't change—but I felt his attention sharpen.

"You did some work in his unit, right?"

"Yeah," Ray said. "Standard stuff."

"Before he disappeared."

"I think so."

"And after."

There it was—a fraction of a pause. Barely measurable. But real.

"Yeah."

I kept my voice neutral. Curious.

"What were you doing in there after he was gone?"

Ray didn't bristle. Didn't dodge.

"Checking the plumbing. Making sure nothing was leaking. Gareth asked me to."

I held his gaze. "Gareth asked you to."

"Yeah."

That name carried weight now.

"Did you ever see Thomas after you went in the first time?"

"No."

"Did Gareth ask you to do anything else in Mr. Keene's apartment, other than checking the plumbing?"

"No."

That answer came too quickly.

Which was what made it dangerous.

I nodded once. “Okay. That’s all I needed.”

Ray didn’t move right away. His eyes stayed on me, trying to read how much I knew.

“I’ll go take care of that work order.”

He left.

I stayed seated, perfectly still.

Ray had access.

Ray had timing.

And Ray had been operating under Gareth’s instructions.

And Ray now knew something else.

I wasn’t Gareth.

I wasn’t naïve.

And I was paying attention.

# CHAPTER 17

AFTER RAY LEFT, I was hoping things would settle down a little. The work day would come to an end, and I could do some long-overdue grocery shopping. It didn't happen that way.

I was still in my office, door open, half-listening to the low hum of the building, when the man stepped into the main office. He wasn't one of the regulars who drifted in to complain about noise or trash or neighbors. He stood just inside the threshold, taking in the space like he was making sure he had the right place.

Mara looked up first.

"Hi," she said. "How can we help you?"

The man took off his cap and held it in both hands. He was older—late sixties, maybe more—but there was nothing fragile about him. He had the build of someone who had worked with his body for a long time, shoulders still square, posture still upright. The lines in his face looked earned, not soft.

"My name's Victor Hale," he said. "I live on nine."

That was when I shifted in my chair.

Ninth floor meant one of the long-term tenants. People who didn't churn. People who noticed patterns.

I looked at his file in the resident database. Apartment 912. Retired electrician. Widower. Lived here eight years.

A man who noticed things because there wasn't much else in his world not to notice.

"What seems to be the problem, Mr. Hale?" Mara asked.

He hesitated. Not nervously—carefully.

"It's my neighbor," he said. "Across the hall. Apartment nine-thirteen. Sofia Alvarez."

I pulled up her name from the resident database.

Sofia Alvarez. Mid-thirties. Freelance graphic designer. Quiet. Paid on time. No complaints. One red flag: She was an AESS subsidy recipient.

"Is she causing a disturbance?" Mara asked.

"No," Victor said. "That's not the problem."

Mara frowned. "I'm not sure I follow."

"She hasn't come or gone in three days."

That got my attention.

I stood up and stepped out into the main office. "Three days?" I asked.

Victor turned toward me. "I'm sorry—"

"I'm Kate," I said. "The new superintendent."

His face softened a little. Not relief—recognition. Authority.

"Ms. Alvarez lives right across from me," he said. "These doors aren't quiet. You hear them. You know when someone leaves, when they come back. She goes out at least once a day. Sometimes twice."

"And you haven't heard her?" I asked.

"Not once. Not her door opening. Not her door closing. Nothing."

Mara glanced at me. "She could just be away."

Victor shook his head. "She doesn't travel. And she always tells me when she's going to be gone. Just a courtesy thing. We've been neighbors a long time."

"Has anyone else been going in or out of her apartment?" I asked.

"No," he said. "That's what made me come down. I kept waiting for someone to show up. A friend. A building employee. Anyone. But nothing."

I felt something tighten in my chest.

"Thank you for telling us," I said. "We'll look into it."

Mara nodded, already reaching for her notepad. "Yes, we'll check on her."

Victor didn't move.

"I just didn't want it to go on any longer," he said. "You start telling yourself you're imagining things. But three days is three days."

"You did the right thing," I said.

He finally nodded and turned back toward the door.

As it closed behind him, the office felt quieter than it had a moment before.

Not peaceful.

Empty.

I went back into my office and stared at Sofia Alvarez's name on the screen.

Across the hall from a man who noticed when doors stopped opening.

Another silence inside the building.

And now it was on my watch.

The ninth floor was quiet in the way only upper floors ever were—no foot traffic, no doors opening and closing, just the distant hum of elevators and the soft, mechanical breathing of the building itself.

Apartment 913 was halfway down the hall.

I took out the master key.

Even after everything I'd already seen—Keene, Rosen, Morales—it still felt wrong sliding it into someone else's lock. A private life, opened with a tool that erased the need for permission.

The door gave with a soft click.

Inside, the air was still.

Not stale. Not abandoned.

Paused.

A coffee mug sat on the tiny kitchen table, half full. A phone charger trailed from an outlet to the edge of the kitchen counter, empty of its phone but still plugged in, still waiting. A jacket lay draped over the back of a chair, as if she'd shrugged it off for just a minute. Shoes sat neatly by the door.

No suitcase.

No open closet.

No signs of someone preparing to go anywhere.

Sofia hadn't packed.

She hadn't planned.

She had stepped out of her life without meaning to leave it.

I moved slowly, keeping my hands to myself, letting my eyes do the work. This wasn't like the other apartments—months cold, layers of dust and abandonment. This one was warm. Lived in. A day interrupted mid-sentence.

The couch still held the faint indentation of someone who'd been sitting there not long ago. A half-folded throw blanket lay across one arm. A laptop sat closed on the coffee table.

Normal.

Too normal.

My chest tightened in that familiar way—the moment when observation gives way to something else. When the investigator realizes she isn't just looking backward anymore.

This was happening now.

Somewhere, something was still moving.

I stood in the center of the room and let the truth settle in.

Another tenant.

Another erased life.

Only this time, I was the one who had to decide what to do about it.

I backed out and locked the door, sliding the master key back into my pocket.

The time had come to visit the Westbridges.

# CHAPTER 18

I WENT BACK TO the office first.

Not because I needed to — but because I wanted to see Mara's reaction when I told her.

Mara looked up when I stepped through the door.

"Sofia Alvarez is definitely missing," I said.

Her pen paused in mid-stroke. "Do you want me to call the Westbridges?"

"No," I said. "I'll take care of it."

She nodded too quickly.

I left the office, figuring she'd be on the phone to the Westbridges before I even reached my car.

The Camelback Corridor was all glass and stone and curated success — law firms, financial firms, family offices tucked behind tasteful signage. The Westbridges' building sat right in the middle of this exclusive part of town: expensive without being flashy, quiet without being empty.

I was almost there when I noticed the car.

A dark gray Lexus ES.

It had been behind me for three lights.

I made a quick right where I didn't need to.

It turned too.

I slowed. It slowed.

I made a tight left into a side street, circled a block, came back out onto Camelback.

The Lexus was still there.

When I pulled into the Westbridges' parking lot, it didn't follow me in. It rolled past the entrance, steady and unhurried, as if it had only been passing by.

It hadn't.

Their office was exactly as I remembered it — polished floors, quiet voices, art that meant money. When I gave my name to the receptionist, she didn't look surprised. Told me to go right in.

"Where to?" I asked.

"The conference room," she said, assuming I remembered how to get there. After all, it had been less than a week since I interviewed there for the job.

They were ready for me.

Which told me Mara had already made the call.

I wasn't ushered in.

I was expected.

Mark and Elaine Westbridge sat at the conference table the way people do when they're used to being listened to. Calm. Controlled. Busy.

No sign of alarm.

No sign of relief.

No sign of anything unexpected.

"Kate," Elaine Westbridge said. "What brings you in?"

I didn't tell them.

I sat down.

Watched.

Their eyes were on me, attentive but not anxious.

Which meant they knew why I was there.

Finally, I said, “A tenant appears to be missing.”

There it was.

The moment.

Their faces barely shifted. They weren’t even trying to act surprised.

“How long?” Elaine asked.

“At least three days.”

Mark Westbridge shook his head. “That’s too soon to assume anything.”

Legal.

Not human.

I nodded, as if considering that.

“Are you going to file a missing-person report with the police?” I asked.

“That’s your responsibility,” Mark countered.

That was revealing.

They weren’t refusing.

They were avoiding ownership.

“Are you going to notify AESS?” I asked.

This time, they hesitated.

“How long has the tenant been gone?” Elaine asked, as if I hadn’t just told them.

“About three days.”

“That would be premature,” she said. “We’d need confirmation.”

“From who?”

“The police.”

That was a surprise.

Did they want me to go to the police?

I leaned back slightly.

"Is that how you handled the three other missing tenants?"

A flicker.

Not panic.

Recognition.

"What tenants?" Mr. Westbridge asked.

"Thomas Keene. Lila Rosen. Javier Morales."

I gave them the timelines.

Eight months. Thirteen months. Almost three.

They stared at me.

Real surprise this time.

"We had no idea," Mrs. Westbridge said.

I didn't argue.

"So you didn't order their apartments sealed?"

"No."

"You didn't instruct Gareth Cole to keep those units untouched?"

"No."

I watched them carefully.

They weren't lying.

Or they were lying very well.

"Did you report Gareth Cole missing?" I asked.

"Why would we?" Mark said. "He resigned."

My spine went cold.

"We have his resignation letter on file," Elaine added.

Of course they did.

I stood.

As I did, my blazer shifted.

The Glock was visible.

Just for a second.

Long enough.

They saw it.

Neither of them commented.

Which was worse than if they had.

I walked out.

If they were guilty, they had erased their tracks.

If they were innocent, someone had built a system designed to keep them blind.

Either way...

The Ashford wasn't just eating people.

It was being managed. And not by me. Maybe not by them.

But now they knew I wasn't just a superintendent.

I was armed.

And I was not going away.

The Camelback Corridor slid past my windshield in a sweep of glass towers and palm-lined medians, people stepping out of coffee shops, crossing streets, going about their day as if nothing was wrong.

The January sky was flawless.

Seventy degrees. Blue. Sharp with light.

Phoenix in winter always lies this way—sunlit, open, unthreatening—like a city that wants you to believe nothing bad ever happens here.

I didn't believe it for a second.

I kept one eye on the rearview mirror as I drove, half-expecting to see the same dark sedan again. Nothing followed me out of the Westbridge lot. No slow crawl.

No careful distance. Just traffic and sunlight and the low hum of the city.

Still, my body stayed tight.

I replayed the meeting as I headed south toward The Ashford.

The Westbridges' faces when I named the other tenants.

The way surprise had flickered—real, not staged.

Their denial.

The resignation letter.

They didn't look like masterminds.

They looked like people who'd been managing a building while someone else quietly hollowed it out from the inside.

Pawns, not kings.

I thought about calling the police.

That was what a normal person would do.

That was what the rules said.

But I knew how it would go.

The moment I filed a report, the case would stop being mine. Detectives would step in, take statements, make notes, ask polite questions. I would become "the building manager." Not the investigator. Not the woman who had already walked through four empty apartments and seen the same pattern repeating itself.

And they wouldn't solve it.

They'd knock on doors.

They'd check phone records.

They'd fill out forms.

But this wasn't a crime that lived in a hallway.

It lived in bank transfers.

In automated payments.

In quiet digital movements that never left fingerprints.

The police don't hunt ghosts in ledgers.

I do.

Javier Morales's account was sitting there, live and untouched, wired to alert me the second someone tried to move the money.

The trap was set.

All I had to do was not scare off whoever was about to walk into it.

Same with AESS.

I could report the missing tenants now. I could blow the whole thing open. But it would collapse the tunnel just as I was finally seeing light at the end of it.

So I kept both weapons where they were.

The police.

AESS.

I'd use them when it mattered.

Not yet.

I made the final turn.

The Ashford rose ahead of me—concrete and glass, quiet and patient.

Waiting.

I walked back into the office like nothing was wrong.

Mara looked up from her desk. "Hey. How did it go?"

I let the question sit there for a beat.

"How did what go?" I asked.

She blinked. "Your meeting. With the Westbridges."

I studied her.

"I didn't tell you where I was going."

Her fingers tightened around her pen. Just slightly.

"They... called," she said. "Just said you were on your way back."

"Why would they do that?"

For a moment, it looked like something real might come out of her.

Her mouth opened.

Then closed.

"I don't know," she said.

I nodded, as if I believed her.

I didn't.

I went into my office and left the door open.

The afternoon slid back into routine.

A tenant came in about a leaky faucet.

Another about a noisy neighbor.

Mara took notes.

Called Ray.

Normal.

Mundane.

Exactly what the building was supposed to feel like when nothing was wrong.

I answered emails.

Reviewed maintenance logs.

Signed off on a lease renewal.

All of it background noise.

My real attention was on one thing.

The burner phone in my pocket.

Based on everything I knew, this should be the day.

Minutes passed.

Then an hour.

The building hummed around me.

Somewhere, a dryer spun.
An elevator chimed.
A door slammed.
And then—
A vibration.
Soft.
Short.
Intimate.
I didn't move.
Didn't reach for it.
Didn't even breathe.
Because I knew exactly what it meant.
Someone, somewhere, had just touched the money.

# CHAPTER 19

I DIDN'T LOOK AT the phone.

Not when I left the office. Not in the elevator. Not even when I stepped into the hallway outside my penthouse and felt the quiet close around me like a door.

I pulled my key out and moved it to the lock.

The deadbolt was new—fresh metal, installed days ago—yet the faceplate bore faint scratches that hadn't been there when the locksmith tightened the last screw. Not gouges. Not a crowbar. Just thin, impatient marks, like someone had tested it with the wrong tool and didn't care what it left behind.

Some people would have frozen.

Backed away, pulled out the phone, called someone, made noise.

I didn't.

I slid my key in and turned it. The deadbolt clicked open with a clean, obedient sound that didn't match what my gut was telling me.

I stepped inside, closed the door, and locked it again.

Still didn't look at the phone.

Instead, I went where I'd left my laptop.

The table beside the kitchen was exactly as it had been. The chair pulled out at the same angle. The closed computer sitting like a silent witness. On the surface, nothing had changed.

That was the point.

People who entered places they didn't belong in didn't throw pillows. They didn't rearrange furniture. They didn't leave calling cards. They left you the illusion of normal so you would keep living inside it.

I slowed my breathing. Slowed my eyes.

I scanned the ceiling first. Corners. Vents. The edges of smoke detectors. Then the walls. Then the objects that were easy to ignore because they belonged in a staged, expensive life.

Art.

I moved closer to the framed flower print on the wall behind the table. It was harmless décor—one of the pieces the Westbridges' assistant had chosen when she'd stocked the place, along with the white towels and the matching soap dispensers and the coffee pods that tasted like nothing.

The frame was thin and matte-black.

And on the lower right corner—where shadow collected—there was a tiny bump that didn't belong.

I leaned in until my breath fogged the glass.

A lens so small you could pretend it was part of the texture if you wanted to keep believing.

I didn't want to keep believing.

I hooked a fingernail under the edge of the frame and pulled. The device popped free with a soft snap.

Lightweight. Cheap plastic. The kind of thing you could order in a pack of five and hide in anything.

My throat tightened—not with fear, exactly. With something colder.

Someone wanted eyes inside my apartment.

And even though I'd cleaned the place once and changed the lock, they'd tried again.

Nice try.

Not good enough.

I carried the device into the bathroom and dropped it in the toilet. It looked ridiculous sitting there for half a second—this tiny black eye in a bowl of clean water—then I flushed.

It disappeared with the swirl like it had never existed.

I watched until the water went still.

Then I walked back out to the table, pulled the chair in, and finally took the phone out of my pocket.

The screen lit up.

A text alert.

Simple. Clinical. The kind of message designed to make you act fast without thinking.

New device login
Location: Phoenix, AZ
Device: Windows PC — Chrome
Time: 3:14 PM

I stared at it for a beat too long.

Not because I didn't understand it.

Because I did.

Someone had gotten into Javier Morales's account.

Not tomorrow. Not next week. Not "any day now." They'd done it today—while I was still downstairs pretending to be normal, while the building hummed and tenants complained about faucets and Mara smiled and wrote things down like none of us were standing on top of a crime scene.

My pulse stayed steady. My body had already made its choice. This wasn't panic time.

This was work.

I took off my blazer and hung it on the back of the chair. The weight of the Glock on my hip was comforting in a way I didn't like to admit. Not because I expected to shoot someone in my kitchen, but because it reminded me I wasn't the kind of person who waited to be rescued.

Then I opened my laptop.

The screen glowed to life, casting a faint light across my hands.

I navigated to the bank's website.

The login screen loaded cleanly.

I entered Javier's username.

Password.

Enter.

The dashboard appeared instantly.

No security prompt. No extra verification. No text code. No "Is this you?"

Which told me everything about the man who'd taped his credentials to his refrigerator door: he trusted routine. He trusted that the world stayed in the lanes it was supposed to stay in.

And it told me something about the person who'd

logged in at 3:14 PM: they hadn't struggled. They hadn't guessed. They hadn't tripped an alarm by failing.

They had the log-on credentials.

And they knew exactly what to do with them.

I clicked Activity.

A list appeared—sessions, timestamps, durations.

There it was near the top.

A new session. Fifteen minutes ago. Duration: just under a minute.

Long enough to change one thing.

Not long enough to browse.

Not long enough to get curious.

They weren't snooping.

They were executing.

I clicked Automatic Payments.

The page loaded with a familiar neatness: payees, scheduled dates, recurring amounts.

The old payment was still there—Westbridge Property Management—but it was grayed out.

Canceled.

A second line sat beneath it, bright and new, like a fresh track laid over an old one.

New Payee Added

Bank: North Meridian Private Bank

First payment scheduled: end of February

My mouth went dry.

They hadn't moved money yet. Not today. Not this minute.

They'd just rerouted the river.

Which meant two things:

One, the system was still operating exactly the way it

had with Keene and Rosen—quietly, predictably, with a three-month fuse.

And two, they didn't know anyone was watching.

Good.

I clicked Payment History.

The last payment to Westbridge had been received yesterday.

The third payment.

Right at the end of January.

Three months after Javier had gone missing.

Javier had been right on the edge of being erased the way the others had been erased—cleanly, administratively, with no sound.

I sat back for a moment, letting the information settle into place.

This wasn't a theory. It wasn't an anxious narrative I'd constructed because the building felt wrong.

It was a process.

An algorithm with a human face.

And today, someone had stepped in to complete the handoff.

I pushed forward before my mind could spin.

I clicked into Security Settings.

Then Login History.

Most people never looked there. Most people assumed the bank was either safe or it wasn't. They didn't think about the trail that every session left behind, the crumbs that technology dropped for anyone disciplined enough to follow them.

I was disciplined enough.

A table appeared:

Date. Time. Browser. Operating system. Location. The newest line was at the top.

Login #1247
Device: Desktop
Browser: Chrome
OS: Windows
Location: Phoenix, AZ

Phoenix was broad. Phoenix was nothing. Phoenix was the entire sprawl—millions of people under the same sun, driving past each other without ever touching.

A VPN could fake Phoenix.

A careful person would fake Phoenix.

So I clicked Details.

A sub-panel slid open.

IP address.

Network provider.

Device signature.

And there, in plain text, was the part that made my spine go rigid.

The address wasn't masked.

No tunnel. No obfuscation. No effort to hide.

Just a raw, institutional network.

I copied the IP address.

Opened a lookup tool.

Pasted.

Hit Enter.

The page loaded slowly enough for the seconds to become loud.

Then the result appeared.

Phoenix, AZ
Network Provider: AESS
Device: Windows PC – Chrome
IP: not masked

For a moment, I didn't move.

The room didn't change. The air conditioning still whispered through vents. The city still shone outside the glass. Somewhere in the building, someone ran water. Someone shut a door. Someone laughed at a television.

Life continued as if the sentence on my screen wasn't a confession.

AESS.

Arizona Emergency Support Services.

The program name I'd seen in files so many times before.

The name I'd heard out of Mara's mouth like it was normal.

The acronym that had lived in the margins of my AG case and would have become the center—except I'd been removed before I could drag it into daylight.

I stared at the screen until the letters blurred slightly.

Not because I was surprised.

Because it was worse than an outside thief.

Worse than a faceless hacker.

Outside criminals were a known quantity. You could imagine them. You could build defenses around them. You could tell yourself they were rare.

This wasn't rare.

This was the engine itself.

The agency that was supposed to be keeping people from falling was reaching into their accounts and moving money with the confidence of someone who knew they'd never be questioned.

It wasn't a hacker in a dark apartment.

It wasn't North Meridian acting alone.

It was coming from inside the system that paid the rent.

Which meant the fraud wasn't riding on the program.

The program was powering it.

My fingers stayed on the edge of the laptop, but I could feel the shift in my body—the same internal click I'd felt years ago in conference rooms and interviews and quiet offices when the truth finally took a shape that couldn't be denied.

I'd been fired before I could confront them.

I'd been silenced before I could put a name to the hand on the lever.

Now the hand had shown itself.

Sloppy. Bold. Confident.

Because why would they bother hiding?

Who was going to look?

Who, outside of law enforcement, was going to believe a missing tenant mattered enough to trace?

I sat back slowly, letting the cold settle in.

The penthouse felt larger than it should have. Quiet in a way that wasn't peaceful. The kind of quiet that made you aware of every blind spot.

They had already broken into my apartment.

They had already put a camera on my wall.

And now, somewhere in Phoenix, someone at AESS had reached into Javier Morales's account and rerouted the money like they were changing an address on a form.

My next move was suddenly obvious—and it wasn't digital.

Now I had the chance I'd been denied.

Now I could confront AESS.

And I would.

# CHAPTER 20

I DIDN'T TOUCH THE keyboard.

The screen was still glowing, the numbers still alive, but I wasn't looking at them anymore. I stood in the middle of my penthouse, hands loose at my sides, as if moving too quickly might crack whatever had just taken shape in my head.

Arizona Emergency Support Services.

The words kept repeating, not on the screen now but inside me. AESS. Not a shell company. Not a crooked bank. Not even a rogue contractor.

A state emergency system.

That single fact rewrote everything.

The Ashford wasn't the engine. It was a mouth. A collection box. A place where people were gathered, sorted, and quietly emptied out.

The money originated in a government pipeline designed to help people who had already fallen through every other crack. Elderly. Disabled. Mentally ill. The kinds of people who could vanish and be explained away with a single line in a database.

Deceased. Transferred. No longer eligible.

Except the missing people weren't being explained away. They weren't being acknowledged at all.

An emergency safety net was being used as a hunting ground.

The Ashford wasn't hiding the crime. It was where the crime was processed.

And I was standing inside it.

That was the part that tightened my chest. Not fear — recognition. I had live access to two of the victim's accounts. I knew the bank where the money was going. And I knew where that bank was routing it. Luxembourg. And now I knew for sure that someone inside AESS was involved.

No one else on the right side of the law had that picture.

Once you saw a machine like that, there was no such thing as pretending you could step away from it.

I left The Ashford and drove east, back toward a part of Phoenix that still felt like mine.

The streets changed as I went — fewer towers, more trees, older buildings, the grid I knew by muscle memory. My old neighborhood sat just south of Camelback, quiet and expensive in a way that tried not to draw attention to itself. The kind of place people moved to when they wanted to disappear into something respectable.

I parked near a narrow storefront with no neon and no gimmicks.

Spy Shop.

It didn't look like anything conspicuous. That was the point.

Inside, the air was cool and still. Glass cases lined the walls, not full of toys or gadgets but of small, serious objects — things designed to listen, to watch, to track. The kind of tools people bought when they didn't want to guess.

I told the clerk what I needed.

A pinhole camera. Wi-Fi capable. Battery powered.

He nodded once and disappeared into the back.

What he brought out fit easily in the palm of my hand. The lens was barely larger than the tip of a pen. The camera body itself was no bigger than a coin, flat and dark, with a thin cable trailing from it. He added a small wireless transmitter and a slim battery pack.

No sales pitch. No questions.

I paid and left.

Back at The Ashford, I crossed the hallway to the framed print opposite my door. It was a good one — abstract, expensive, the kind of thing people bought because someone else had told them it was art.

I took it down and removed the backing.

I made a pinhole in the print where the camera would blend in seamlessly. I pressed it into the pinhole, checking to make sure it would hold. The transmitter and battery fit behind the frame, hidden by the matting and the wall.

When I put the picture back up, it was just that — a picture.

I activated the software on my phone and the image of my front door appeared.

The feed came up clean. Hallway, carpet, my own door centered in the frame. Anyone who came or went would be recorded, whether they knew it or not.

Two could play this game.

I went back into my apartment and packed.

Everything I'd brought with me when I moved in.

If someone could pick my lock and enter without leaving a trace, The Ashford wasn't safe anymore. It was just another controlled space.

I would go back to my apartment and stay there until the lease ran out at the end of February.

It seemed unlikely to me at that moment that I'd be coming back to live in the penthouse apartment.

When I stepped out into the hall, I glanced once at the picture across from my door.

From the outside, it was just art.

From the inside, it was watching me leave.

# CHAPTER 21

I LEFT MY APARTMENT around 9 a.m. the next morning and drove west on Camelback, turned south on Central, and followed it downtown, then turned west again.

The city peeled away in layers. First, the glass and money of Midtown, then the hospitals and clinics, then the low-rise government buildings that all looked as if they'd been designed by the same exhausted committee. The streets grew wider. The intersections farther apart. Concrete replaced polish. Bureaucracy replaced ambition.

I kept an eye on the clock.

It took me fifteen minutes to get there.

No tails. Maybe they were already there, waiting for me in the parking lot.

The AESS complex sat back from the road behind a sweep of parking lot and beige concrete, one of those multi-agency state campuses that tried to look welcoming and ended up looking institutional. Flagpoles out front. Glass doors. A security desk visible through the glare.

I parked, got out, opened my center console, and put my gun inside. Left the holster on my belt.

Then I walked in unarmed.

Inside, the air smelled faintly of disinfectant and tired carpet. Fluorescent lights hummed. A line of people waited in front of a reception window, clutching folders and forms. Beyond that were badge-controlled doors and narrow corridors.

Security waved me forward. My bag went on a belt. I stepped through a metal detector. It stayed silent. A guard gave me a quick wand sweep anyway, then nodded me on.

I was inside their house now.

At reception, I leaned in just enough to be heard.

"I'm the superintendent for The Ashford. I need to speak to the case officer assigned to our building. There's a payment discrepancy tied to an AESS tenant file."

The receptionist pulled something up on her screen. Her fingers moved, paused, moved again.

"Have a seat," she said.

I waited.

A man in a wrinkled button-down eventually appeared and called my name. He led me through a badge-operated door, down a corridor, and into a small conference room with a dry-erase board and a box of tissues.

I sat.

"One of your recipients," I said, then stopped, to let that sit with him. "Has been gone for eight months. AESS is still paying them."

He barely looked up. "It happens."

No alarm. No curiosity. He didn't even ask how I knew.

After a moment, he said, "What's the name?"

"I'm not giving it to you."

He frowned. "Why not?"

"Because you don't seem to care," I said. "I'd like to speak to your supervisor."

"That's not necessary."

"It is."

He stared at me, then stood and left.

The supervisor who came back with him was a different animal. Calm. Pressed. Precise.

He was in his mid-thirties, with closely-cropped brown hair.

"My colleague has brought me up to speed on your missing tenant. What was his name again?"

"I think you know his name," I said.

He raised his eyebrows, tilted his head to the side, like it didn't matter if he knew or not.

"He's been missing for eight months, and AESS is still paying him. Why?"

He didn't answer. But he didn't deny any of it. Just nodded his head and looked straight into my eyes. I looked right back.

"What's your name?" I asked.

He hesitated, then gave it. "Thomas Kline."

"Can you spell that, please?"

He spelled his last name.

My eyes remained locked on his.

"And your title?"

"Senior Manager, Emergency Benefits Operations."

I smiled. "Thank you."

"If you give us the names," he said, "we'll look into it."

That was interesting. He asked for "names," but I'd only mentioned one person was missing.

"They're in my car."

"I'll accompany you."

That was the moment I knew he was part of it.

"No," I said. "I'll be right back."

I left before he could argue.

The parking lot felt too open after the fluorescent corridors. I got into my car and drove.

Five minutes. Ten.

At a wide intersection a black SUV blew through a red light and hit me broadside.

The impact was violent and sideways. Airbags exploded. Glass burst. Pain bloomed across my chest and shoulder.

I was injured and dazed, but not so badly that I couldn't figure out this wasn't an accident.

I unlatched my seatbelt, grabbed my gun from the console, lurched over, and pushed the passenger door open. I crawled out, my ribs screaming, and landed on the pavement. Rolled onto my back.

A man in a black hoodie was already coming around the hood of the SUV, a gun in his hand.

I fired. Three times.

He went down hard.

I heard the car door of the SUV that had rammed me slam shut. Then screeching tires, the engine revving high as the other assailant made a run for it.

Sirens were already rising.

I slid down to the pavement and waited, my back against the rear door of the car.

Now I knew for sure.

Whoever was behind this would kill to protect themselves.

I doubted it was Thomas Kline.

But he would lead me to them.

I stayed where I was.

Seated on the pavement, my back against the rear door of my car, one knee bent, the other stretched out awkwardly in front of me. The metal was still warm. The smell of burned rubber and something sweeter—coolant, maybe—hung in the air.

People were everywhere.

It was a busy intersection. I'd clocked that the second I rolled out of the car. Cars stopped at odd angles. Drivers half out of their seats. A small knot of people on the sidewalk, phones raised, filming openly. No one shouting. Just that strange, held-breath quiet that comes after violence, when everyone knows something irreversible has happened but hasn't figured out what to do with it yet.

My head rang. Not pain exactly—more like pressure. A low-frequency hum behind my eyes. I tested it gently, rolling my shoulders, taking inventory. Ribs hurt. Left side worse than right. No sharp spikes when I breathed, which was good. My hands were steady enough. That mattered.

I needed them steady.

A man came up to me as the sirens approached.

Mid-forties, maybe. Button-down shirt, sleeves rolled. He'd stopped a few feet away, palms open.

"You okay?" he'd asked. "I saw the whole thing."

"You should step back. Over there." I nodded toward the curb. "They're going to want statements."

He hesitated, then did what I said.

The sirens arrived fast. Multiple units. Phoenix PD doesn't take chances with scenes like this.

Squad cars slid in from every direction, blocking the intersection completely. Doors flew open. Guns came up.

I didn't move.

I placed my weapon on the ground beside me, carefully, grip facing away, then raised my hands as high as my ribs would allow.

One of the officers approached, weapon still trained on me. He stopped short, eyes flicking between me, the gun on the pavement, the body near the intersection.

"I'm former PPD," I said, loud enough to carry but not a shout. "My name is Katherine Mercer."

No acknowledgment. Just commands.

"Hands up. Don't move."

I raised my hands as far as I could, but the pain in my shoulder and ribs kept them low.

"I'm injured," I said. "I can't put my hands behind my back."

He glanced back at his partner, said something low I couldn't hear. Then: "We're going to cuff you in front. For officer safety. Turn your palms out."

I did.

The cuffs clicked closed around my wrists. Cold metal. Familiar weight. I focused on breathing evenly, keeping my vision steady. The concussion made everything feel half a step delayed, as if the world around me were being filtered through a glass. I couldn't let that show.

I couldn't lose control now. Not after AESS. Not after finally seeing the shape of it.

I saw the bystander who'd approached me earlier—one of the officers had him off to the side, asking questions. Good. That helped me. I wasn't just a woman with a gun and a dead man at her feet. I was a victim with witnesses. Also a suspect. Both things could be true at once.

An officer knelt near the man I'd shot. Checked for a pulse. Checked again.

"He's gone," he said.

That was the moment the air changed.

Radios crackled. Voices sharpened. Someone pulled yellow tape from a trunk.

I watched it all from the pavement, hands cuffed in front of me, head humming, the weight of it settling in.

I'd killed a man.

This was now a homicide investigation.

# CHAPTER 22

THE AMBULANCE ARRIVED not long after the police had secured the scene.

I heard it before I saw it—the siren, the diesel rumble, the muted hiss of brakes. The crowd had been pushed back by then. Yellow tape fluttered at the edges of my vision. The intersection no longer belonged to the public. It belonged to uniforms.

Two EMTs approached with a wheeled stretcher. Efficient. Moving fast but giving the impression of being unhurried. They'd done this a thousand times before.

One of them crouched in front of me. "Can you tell me where you're hurting?"

"My ribs," I said. "Left side. My shoulder. And my head."

He nodded, already reaching for the blood pressure cuff. Another hand slipped the pulse oximeter onto my finger. The cuff tightened, released. Tightened again.

"No loss of consciousness?"

"No."

"Nausea?"

"No."

"Any trouble breathing?"

"Not yet."

They moved me carefully, one on each side, lifting just enough to slide me onto the gurney. The metal frame creaked softly. Straps came next—chest, legs—snug but not tight. A soft collar was placed around my neck, more precaution than necessity, but I didn't argue. This wasn't the moment.

As they rolled me toward the ambulance, I caught a glimpse of the man I'd shot. Covered now. No movement beneath the sheet.

Inside the ambulance, the world narrowed.

Fluorescent lights. Cabinets lining the walls. The low, constant beep of a monitor syncing to my pulse. The rear doors closed behind us with a solid, final thud.

One of the EMTs climbed in with me, taking a position at my side. The other moved to the front.

A uniformed officer followed and sat on the bench along the wall and fastened his seatbelt. His weapon was holstered. Radio clipped to his shoulder.

Not guarding me.

Not comforting me.

Just there.

The ambulance pulled away from the curb. I felt the slight sway as we merged into traffic, the familiar rhythm of city streets giving way to smoother pavement. I recognized the route almost immediately.

They were taking me to Banner University Medical Center.

This area of town, of course it would be Banner.

The EMT checked my pupils, brief and professional. Pressed gently along my ribs. Watched my face for tells.

"Let me know if your pain changes," he said. "Or if you feel dizzy."

"I will."

The officer didn't speak.

I stared up at the ceiling and focused on keeping my thoughts ordered. On staying sharp. The concussion made everything feel dulled around the edges, like the city was being filtered through glass, but the core of it was still there.

I'd walked into AESS and forced them to react.

I wasn't going to lose that now.

The ambulance slowed, turned. Backed into the bay.

The doors opened, and cooler air touched my face. Hands unlocked the gurney. Wheels rolled again.

As they transferred me from the ambulance to the hospital gurney, the officer stood and followed without comment.

I was no longer on the street.

I was inside the system.

And the system was coming for me.

Again.

They rolled me into the emergency department through a set of sliding doors that opened without hesitation.

The sound changed immediately. Sirens and traffic fell away, replaced by overlapping voices, the squeak of rubber soles on polished floors, the constant low noise of machines doing their jobs. The air smelled different too—cleaner, sharper, layered with antiseptic and something metallic beneath it.

Hands took over.

Not the EMTs anymore. New people. New gloves. Someone called out my name before I was fully inside the room, and someone else repeated it, louder, as if that made it official.

A nurse cut away part of my shirt without asking. Another set of hands pressed adhesive pads to my chest. Leads snapped into place. The bed locked with a dull clunk.

"Any allergies?"

"No."

"Loss of consciousness at the scene?"

"No."

"Nausea?"

"No."

"Pain level?"

I took a second to inventory it honestly. The pressure behind my eyes. The ache in my ribs every time I breathed in too deeply. The dull burn along my shoulder where the seatbelt had done its job.

"Five," I said. Then, after a beat, "Six."

That earned a nod. Not concern. Data logged.

They moved quickly, but not urgently. I'd spent enough years around emergency rooms to know the difference. If they were worried, the room would feel different. Tighter. Louder. Instead, this was controlled.

A portable X-ray machine was wheeled in beside the bed. It looked like a squat metal insect on wheels. They positioned my arms carefully, told me when to inhale, when to hold it. The machine hummed, clicked, and was gone again.

“Any pain here?” Fingers pressed along my ribs.

“Yes.”

“Here?”

“Yes.”

“Sharp or dull?”

“Sharp.”

More notes. More nods.

Later—minutes or maybe longer—they wheeled me down a quieter corridor toward imaging. The ceiling tiles passed overhead in a familiar pattern. I’d watched them before, from the other side of the stretcher, when I was the one standing at the foot of the bed.

The CT scanner waited in a room that felt colder than the rest of the department. They slid me onto the narrow table, adjusted my head, reminded me not to move.

The machine swallowed my vision in a ring of white. A calm voice came over a speaker.

“Hold still. You’ll hear the machine.”

I stared straight up and focused on breathing shallowly. The concussion made everything feel slightly delayed, like my thoughts were arriving a fraction of a second after the world did. I didn’t like that. I compensated by slowing down.

They rolled me into a private room. A nurse cleaned cuts on my forearm and near my collarbone. I watched her work, realizing I hadn’t noticed the injuries at all until that moment. Next, she wiped the dried blood from my hands. That, too, had escaped my attention.

The officer was still there.

Positioned near the door. Same posture. Not leaning. Not pacing. Present without intruding. He spoke quietly with a nurse at one point, then went still again.

He hadn't asked me anything since the ambulance.

That wasn't an oversight.

Time stretched. The edge of the pain dulled as medication took effect, but it didn't disappear. I could feel it waiting underneath, patient. Tomorrow would be worse. I knew that too.

I stayed focused anyway. Counted the beeps of the monitor. Noted footsteps in the hallway. Didn't let my thoughts jump ahead.

A few hours after I'd been brought in, a doctor finally came in to talk to me. About my age, maybe younger. Calm in the way that comes from repetition, not indifference. He flipped through my chart without rushing.

"You're lucky," he said. "No internal bleeding. No collapsed lung."

I waited.

"You've got bruised ribs—possibly a small fracture we won't see right away. Soft-tissue injury to your left shoulder. Mild concussion, but enough to explain what you're feeling. Superficial lacerations from glass."

Nothing disabling. Enough to slow me down.

"No surgery," he continued. "We'll keep you for observation. Pain management. Neurological checks overnight."

He paused, then looked at me directly.

"You're medically cleared to speak," he said. "There are two detectives waiting."

# CHAPTER 23

THEY DIDN'T KNOCK.

The door opened just far enough for two men to step inside, one after the other, without asking permission. The uniform posted himself outside. That was intentional. This wasn't his room anymore.

I was in a hospital bed angled slightly upright, one arm free, the other tethered to a blood-pressure cuff that hissed every few minutes like it was reminding me where I was. The room was small, beige, designed for turnover. No windows. A monitor blinking steadily at my left. A tray table pushed aside, untouched.

They stood near the foot of the bed.

Not close. Not far.

Close enough to control the room. Far enough to keep distance on the record.

Two detectives. Plainclothes. Jackets open, hands visible, posture relaxed in the way that only comes from experience. The older one took the position slightly forward, not by much, just enough to establish hierarchy.

The younger stayed half a step back and to the side, already watching everything—me, the room, his partner.

"Detective Walker," the older one said.

The name landed.

I knew of Jim Walker from my days on the force. Not personally—but I'd seen his name often enough on reports to know exactly who he was. Homicide. Long tenure. Careful reputation. A man who didn't rush and didn't miss much.

"Detective Reyes," the younger one added, already glancing at the chart clipped to the foot of the bed before looking back at me.

Procedure-first. No history. No tells yet.

Walker didn't smile when our eyes met, but there was a flicker of recognition there. Not surprise. Confirmation.

So the background check had already been done. My service record. My years in uniform. My time as a detective. The move to the Attorney General's office. The quieter, messier part that followed.

Walker spoke again.

"Katherine Mercer."

It wasn't a question.

"Yes."

"Date of birth?"

I gave it. Slowly. Clearly. Making sure it landed clean.

He nodded once, like he was checking a box only he could see.

"For the record," he said, "you understand why we're here."

I did.

A man was dead. I had fired the shots. Everything else—intent, context, motive—came later.

"I do," I said.

No sympathy. No accusation.

Just control.

They weren't here to confront me.

They were here to figure out my role in what had happened.

And lying back against the stiff hospital pillow, ribs aching every time I breathed too deeply, I understood something important before the questioning even began:

This room belonged to them now.

Walker didn't sit.

Neither of them did.

That, too, was intentional.

"Before we go any further," Walker said, "we need to make sure you're able to give a statement."

I nodded once. Slow. Deliberate.

"Did you lose consciousness at any point today?" he asked.

"No."

"After the collision?"

"No."

"After the shooting?"

"No."

Reyes glanced at the monitor, then at me. Tracking consistency.

"Are you on any pain medication right now?" Walker asked.

"They gave me something for inflammation," I said. "Nothing narcotic."

Walker's eyes stayed on mine. Not challenging. Verifying.

"Do you feel clearheaded?"

Clearheaded wasn't the word I would've chosen.

My ribs ached every time I breathed. My shoulder felt like it had been wrenched halfway out of its socket. There was a dull pressure behind my eyes, the kind that made the room feel slightly out of sync with itself. But my thoughts were linear. Ordered.

"I'm thinking clearly," I said. "If that's what you're asking."

It was.

Walker nodded again, like he was stacking small bricks into place.

"Do you understand that this conversation is being recorded?"

"Yes."

"And that you're free to stop answering questions at any time?"

"Yes."

Reyes shifted his stance slightly, the way younger detectives do when they're settling into a long interview. He hadn't said much yet, but he was already mapping me. Responses. Cadence. Control.

Walker folded his hands loosely in front of him.

"For the record," he said, "you're not under arrest at this time."

At this time.

"But," he continued, "this is a homicide investigation. Anything you say here will be evaluated in that context."

I didn't respond. I didn't need to.

We all understood what that meant.

Walker held my gaze for another beat, long enough to be sure I wasn't drifting, slurring, or searching for words.

Then he said, "All right."

And just like that, the room shifted.

The preliminaries were done.

What came next would count.

Walker didn't rush into the next question.

He let the silence sit for a moment longer than necessary, watching to see if I'd fill it. I didn't. That used to be one of my strengths. It still was.

He glanced down at his notes—not to read, but to signal a transition.

"Let's get some background on the record," he said. "Your background."

I nodded once.

"Phoenix Police Department," he said. "Eight years in uniform. Seven as a detective."

"Yes."

"Why'd you leave patrol?"

"Promotion," I said. "Detective exam."

Reyes's pen moved. Short strokes. Clean handwriting.

"And after seven years as a detective," Walker continued, "you went to work at the Attorney General's office."

"Yes."

"Why?"

"Better hours," I said. "Different work."

Not untrue. Not complete.

Walker watched my face carefully. Not for the words. For the space around them.

"And you left the AG's office," he said.

That wasn't a question.

"Yes."

"Voluntarily?"

The word landed heavier than it should have.

"No," I said. "They terminated me."

Reyes looked up at that. Just for a second.

Walker didn't.

"Why?"

There it was. Clean. Direct. On the record.

"I violated internal policy," I said.

Walker studied me, weighing whether to press or pivot.

"What policy?"

"I was instructed not to discuss it."

I didn't rush the answer. I didn't hedge it. I didn't dress it up.

It wasn't defiance.

It wasn't evasion.

It was a boundary that had already been drawn.

Walker held my gaze for a moment longer, then nodded once—accepting what he couldn't move today.

"Any disciplinary actions pending at the time?" he asked.

"No."

"Any findings of misconduct?"

"No."

"And no criminal charges?"

"No."

Each answer tightened the room—not because they contradicted him, but because they closed doors he might have wanted to leave open.

Walker tilted his head slightly, studying me in a way that felt familiar. Like a supervisor deciding whether to push harder or change direction.

"You understand," he said, "why your background matters here."

"I do."

"Former detectives don't get the benefit of the doubt," he said evenly. "They get more scrutiny."

I almost smiled at that.

Almost.

"I'd expect nothing less," I said.

Reyes's pen paused. Just briefly.

Walker leaned back a fraction, like he'd just confirmed something he already suspected.

"This isn't an informal conversation," he said. "Everything you say becomes part of a permanent record."

"I know," I said.

"And the fact that you know how this works," he added, "means we'll be holding you to a higher standard."

There it was.

Not a threat.

Not a warning.

A condition.

I met his eyes and didn't look away.

"Fair enough," I said.

Walker studied me for another moment, then nodded once.

"All right," he said. "Let's talk about your day."

And just like that, my past was officially in the room with us.

Walker didn't ask the next question right away.

He shifted his weight slightly, the way men do when they're settling in for something that's going to take a while.

"Let's start at the beginning of your day," he said.

Not why questions.

Not what happened.

Beginning.

"When did you wake up?"

I told him.

"Where were you?"

"At my apartment."

"Alone?"

"Yes."

Reyes's pen moved again. He didn't look up.

Walker kept his voice even. Almost conversational.

"What time did you leave?"

I gave him the time. Approximate, but accurate.

"And where were you headed?"

I paused—just long enough to be human, not long enough to look rehearsed.

"Running errands," I said.

Walker didn't react. He didn't challenge it either.

"What part of town?"

"Central Phoenix."

Reyes glanced up then, briefly, like he was placing a pin on a mental map.

"What errands?" Walker asked.

"Personal," I said. "Nothing unusual."

I knew exactly what I wasn't saying.

If I named the building—if I said AESS out loud—it would stop being my investigation. It would become theirs. Formal. Jurisdictional. Slowed by process and buried under inter-agency review before it ever saw daylight. If it ever saw daylight at all.

So I didn't offer it.

I answered the questions they asked. No more. No less.

It wasn't the same as lying.

It was sequencing.

Walker let my answer sit. He wasn't looking for detail yet. He was establishing how much I would volunteer without pressure.

"Did you stop anywhere?" he asked.

"Yes."

"How many places?"

"A couple."

"What places?"

"Places where you go when you're running errands."

Reyes's pen paused. Restarted.

Walker nodded once, accepting the answer for now. He knew I wasn't going to tell him, so why waste time pushing it.

"And after that?"

"I got back in my car and headed east."

"Where were you going?"

"Back home."

That part was true. Just not the whole truth.

Walker's eyes stayed on my face, tracking cadence more than content.

"Did you notice anyone following you?"

"No."

"Any unusual vehicles?"

"No."

Reyes finally looked up, meeting my eyes for the first time since they'd started.

"You're sure about that?" he asked.

"Yes."

He held my gaze a beat longer than necessary, then looked back down and wrote something anyway.

Walker took the questioning back.

"Tell us about the intersection," he said. "Before the collision."

I described it clinically. Traffic light. Cross street. My speed. Green light. No warning.

"And the impact?" Reyes asked.

"From the driver's side," I said. "Hard. No braking."

Reyes nodded, already building the reconstruction in his head.

"And after the collision?" Walker asked.

"I was disoriented," I said. "But conscious."

"Did you exit the vehicle immediately?"

"Yes."

"How long before the man approached you?"

"Seconds. Less than ten."

Reyes's pen stopped moving.

"Where was he coming from?" he asked.

"From the front of my car."

"And he was armed?"

"Yes."

"With what?"

"A handgun."

Walker let that hang for a moment.

"And what did you do?"

"I shot him."

"Why? Did you feel he was a threat to you?"

"Yes."

"Why?"

"Because his car had just rammed mine—and he had a gun pointed at me."

The room went quiet again.

Walker glanced down at his notes, then back at me.

"Everything you just told us," he said, "or didn't tell us... is going to be checked."

"I know," I said.

"Every location," he continued. "Every stop. Every minute."

I nodded once.

Because this was the part most people didn't understand.

It didn't matter whether I was lying or telling the truth.

What mattered was that I'd just given them a map.

But this map would keep them away from my case.

For now.

## CHAPTER 24

REYES, THE YOUNGER detective, took the lead after that.

They walked through the crash quickly—lanes, light cycle, speed, point of impact. I answered without hesitation. Muscle memory. Training.

He moved on to the shooting just as clinically. Distance. Timing. Where my weapon was. When I drew it. When I fired. How many shots.

Nothing I said surprised them.

When he finally closed his notebook, Walker nodded once.

"So far," he said, "your account matches the physical evidence."

So far.

Walker didn't look down at his notes.

He held my gaze for a beat, then said, "There's something else."

Reyes had gone still beside him, tablet resting against his thigh, stylus unmoving.

"Do you know of any reason someone would be tracking you or your vehicle?" Walker asked.

The question was too calm.

"No," I said.

Walker nodded once.

"During our preliminary processing of your car," he said, "we located a GPS tracking device."

He paused.

"Mounted underneath the frame. Magnetized."

I didn't react right away. I let the silence do the work.

"A tracker?" I said.

"Yes," Reyes said. "Installed cleanly. Whoever put it there knew what they were doing."

"Do you have any idea when?" I asked.

"That's still being determined," Walker said. "But it wasn't placed today."

So this hadn't started with the crash.

Walker watched me carefully now. Not for surprise. For calculation.

"You have any idea who would want to know where you are?" he asked.

"No."

Reyes leaned in slightly. "Anyone you're having a dispute with? Personal. Professional."

"No."

Walker shifted back a fraction, reassessing.

"You understand what this changes," he said.

"Yes."

"It means this wasn't random," Reyes said. "And it wasn't opportunistic."

"I know."

Walker nodded once.

"Which brings us back to motive," he said. "And whether there's something you haven't told us."

I met his eyes and didn't look away.

Because now it wasn't just my timeline they were examining.

It was my silence.

Walker didn't raise his voice.

He didn't need to.

"Ms. Mercer," he said, "people don't put trackers on cars for no reason."

I said nothing.

Reyes shifted his weight, watching me from the corner of his eye. He wasn't impatient. He was waiting for the moment where silence stopped being strategic and started being suspicious.

Walker continued.

"This wasn't random," he said. "Someone knew where you were."

I kept my face neutral. Let him talk.

"And then," he added, "you're hit in an intersection. Hard. Immediately afterward, a man approaches you with a gun."

He let the sequence hang in the air between us.

"That's not coincidence," Walker said. "That's design."

"I agree," I said.

Walker nodded once, like he'd expected that answer.

"So help us understand the design," he said. "Why you?"

There it was.

Not who.

Not how.

Why.

I took a breath. Slow. Measured.

"I don't know," I said.

Reyes looked up sharply. Not because the answer surprised him — because it closed a door.

Walker studied me for a long moment.

"You're a former detective," he said. "You understand how unlikely that sounds."

"I understand how it sounds," I said. "That doesn't make it untrue."

Walker leaned forward slightly now. Not aggressive. Intent.

"Anyone you've been looking into?" he asked. "Anyone who might be unhappy about your attention?"

"No."

That was the first outright lie I'd told. I needed time—long enough to find Kline before someone else did.

"Anyone who might think you were," he pressed.

I met his eyes. Held them.

"If I knew who was watching me," I said, "we wouldn't be having this conversation."

Reyes exhaled quietly through his nose. Amused? Frustrated? Hard to tell.

Walker leaned back again.

"You know what this looks like," he said.

"Yes."

"You know how this reads on paper."

"Yes."

"And you know," he continued, "that withholding

information doesn't make it disappear. It just makes us look for it somewhere else."

I didn't respond.

Walker closed his notebook.

"For now," he said, "we're done with questions."

Reyes straightened slightly. The recorder clicked off. The red light disappeared, and with it the sense that anything left unsaid might still be safe.

Walker didn't sit. He hadn't at any point.

"Your firearm is being held as evidence," he said. "You understand that."

I did.

I'd known it from the moment the words homicide investigation had been spoken aloud.

For half a second, I considered asking anyway. About reminding them it was legally owned. Registered. That the shooting itself would almost certainly be ruled clean.

But I also knew how that would sound.

Like urgency.

Like attachment.

Like someone who wanted her weapon back too badly.

So I didn't ask.

Walker noticed that, too.

"Your vehicle is being processed," he continued. "And your phone will be examined."

Reyes added, "Including location data."

"I assumed as much," I said.

Walker studied me, measuring not what I said — but what I didn't.

"This isn't punishment," he said. "It's containment. Until we understand what we're dealing with."

"And until then?" I asked.

"We don't want you leaving the city."

It wasn't phrased as an order.

It didn't need to be.

I didn't argue. I didn't protest.

Arguing would suggest fear.

Protesting would suggest guilt.

"I understand," I said.

Walker nodded once.

"Good."

Reyes moved toward the door, ready to end it cleanly. Walker stayed where he was, beside my bed, eyes locked on mine.

"This part isn't on the record," he said.

Reyes didn't react. He didn't need to. This wasn't the first time Walker had drawn that line.

Walker lowered his voice — not to hide it, but to narrow it.

"You're smart," he said. "You know how this looks."

"I do."

"And you know what happens when someone keeps pushing after they've been warned."

He wasn't threatening me.

He was reminding me of gravity.

"I'm not telling you to stop," he went on. "That's not my job."

I waited.

"I'm telling you that if this turns into something bigger — and it already feels like it has — you won't get the benefit of the doubt."

"I lost that over a year ago," I said.

"Exactly," he agreed. "Which means every move you make gets read the worst possible way."

Reyes shifted his weight. Enough.

Walker straightened.

"We'll be in touch," he said, laying his card on the side table beside my bed. "Don't make us chase you."

"I won't," I said.

Walker held my gaze one last time.

"You know how this ends," he said quietly.

Yes.

I did.

More than they did.

Eventually, they'd find out where I'd been, and they'd find out why. That was what Walker had been telling me, without telling me. He also realized that wouldn't necessarily make me guilty of murder. But what he didn't understand was that those answers would open up an investigation into AESS that would lead nowhere. Because detectives for PPD had to follow the rules.

I didn't.

They left together. The door closed. The officer outside remained.

I lay back against the pillow, ribs aching, head still humming.

I wasn't under arrest.

I wasn't cleared.

And whatever I was in now had a perimeter —

one that had just been drawn around me.

# CHAPTER 25

BY MORNING, THE hospital was ready to discharge me.

The doctor was brisk. Overnight observation complete. No internal bleeding. No fractures. A mild concussion that would make itself known when it felt like it. He gave me instructions I'd already anticipated—rest, fluids, no driving, follow-up with my primary care doctor in a week—and handed over paperwork clipped together with professional finality.

I nodded and signed where indicated.

When I swung my legs off the bed, my ribs registered the movement immediately. Not sharp. Just firm resistance, like a boundary I'd crossed too quickly. I adjusted the way I stood without thinking about it, rolling one shoulder until it loosened enough to cooperate.

The uniformed officer was gone.

He hadn't been there when I woke up. No one had replaced him. The chair near the door was empty, pushed back where it had been abandoned the night before.

That was its own kind of message.

Free, but not cleared.

I dressed slowly, aware of the stiffness settling in now that adrenaline was no longer doing the work for me. The bruising felt deep enough to be structural, like it belonged to my skeleton instead of my skin. My head carried a low, constant pressure—nothing dramatic, just enough to remind me to move deliberately.

At the discharge desk, the nurse slid a prescription across the counter with the rest of the paperwork. Something stronger than ibuprofen. I glanced at it once, folded it, and slipped it into the pocket of my jacket without comment.

"Could you call me a taxi?" I asked.

She nodded, already reaching for the phone.

Outside, the air was cool and dry. I took a careful breath and felt my ribs answer back. Not pain, exactly. Feedback.

I paused at the curb, steadying myself for a second before moving on.

The city moved as it always had. Cars passed. People walked by without looking at me. No sirens. No watchers I could see.

Whatever perimeter I was inside now, it didn't announce itself.

The taxi pulled up a minute later.

"Biltmore Fashion Park," I said as I slid into the back seat. "On Camelback."

The driver nodded and pulled away from the curb.

The motion tugged at my ribs again—not enough to stop me, just enough to remind me to sit carefully. I adjusted against the seat, found a position that didn't ask too much of my shoulder, and let the city start moving past the windows.

We headed east.

Camelback looked the same as it always had—palms, storefronts, traffic moving with quiet confidence. Midday. People with time. People with money. No one paying attention to anything outside their own errands.

Good.

I watched reflections in the glass as we passed intersections. Habit. The concussion sat behind my eyes like pressure, not pain, sharpening whenever I focused too tightly on anything close. I let my gaze widen instead, took in movement rather than detail.

The driver drove smoothly. No sudden stops. I appreciated that more than I would have yesterday.

By the time Biltmore Fashion Park came into view, the ache in my ribs had settled into something steady and predictable. Manageable.

The taxi pulled up near the main entrance. I paid, thanked him, and stepped out carefully, letting the door close behind me.

The shopping center was already awake—shoppers moving between stores, the low hum of conversations, the clink of coffee cups. Normal life, continuing without interruption.

Inside one of the phone stores, the air was cool and quiet. Bright displays. Neutral walls. A young man behind the counter looked up and smiled the way people did when they expected a transaction, not a story.

"I need a phone," I said. "Basic setup. New number."

No explanations. No hesitation.

He nodded and got to work.

I stayed standing while he did, leaning a fraction of my weight onto my good leg. My shoulder protested softly. I ignored it. This wouldn't take long.

Minutes later, I walked back out into the sunlight with a small bag in my hand and a phone number that didn't exist yesterday.

No history. No contacts. No trail worth following yet.

That would come later.

For now, it was enough to be reachable again—on my terms.

I stepped away from the entrance and paused, letting the movement and noise of the place wash over me. People passed close without looking twice. Conversations overlapped. Cars rolled through the lot in slow, patient arcs.

I knew what I would do next.

I just needed to get back to my apartment to do it.

It was only three blocks away.

So I decided to walk.

The walk took longer than it should have.

Three blocks wasn't much on paper. It was enough in practice. By the time I reached my building, the ache in my ribs had sharpened into something that demanded attention, and my shoulder had gone tight in a way that suggested it would argue with me later. I climbed the stairs anyway, slower than usual, stopping once on the landing to let the pressure in my head settle.

Inside my apartment, I locked the door and stood

there for a moment, breathing carefully, letting the quiet close around me.

Then I went to the bathroom.

The mirror caught me before I could look away. A deep bruise bloomed along my cheekbone, darkening toward my jaw. Another shadowed the bridge of my nose, yellow already edging in at the margins. There were a few small cuts—nothing that would scar, the doctor had said—thin lines already crusted over, more irritating than painful. I looked tired. Older. Not broken, just unmistakably marked.

I opened the cabinet, shook three ibuprofen into my palm, and tried to swallow them dry.

Didn't work.

With the pills stuck in my throat, I crossed to the kitchen, pulled a bottle of water from the fridge, and took a long drink, letting the cold carry the pills down.

The prescription from the hospital was still folded in the pocket of my jacket. Something stronger. I hadn't filled it. I wasn't going to today.

I carried the water bottle to the kitchen table, opened up my laptop, and sat down carefully, shifting until my ribs stopped protesting.

Then I got to work.

I set the small bag with the new phone on the counter and left it there. That could wait.

I opened the browser and logged into the insurance portal.

New claim.

Date.

Time.

Location.

Collision. Police report pending. Vehicle likely totaled.

I submitted the claim and noted the confirmation number. No estimate on payout. No timeline.

I closed the window and moved on.

My bank balance came next. Lower than I liked. Not catastrophic. The first deposit from Westbridge had arrived that morning. I ran the numbers automatically—rent covered, utilities manageable, groceries conservative. Not much left after that.

I accepted the constraint and recalibrated.

No car meant no gas, no insurance payments, no maintenance. Walking cost time and energy. Taxis cost money but left fewer fingerprints than ownership.

For now, I'd decide based on distance and necessity. Now that I had a phone again, Uber was also back on the table.

The pressure behind my eyes eased a fraction as the ibuprofen began to work. Not gone. Just quieter.

Pain was information. It didn't get to make decisions.

I set up the phone next—basic configuration, nothing linked, nothing imported. A number with no history attached to it. When it was done, I set it face down on the table and left it there.

Only then did I open a new browser window and log into Thomas Keene's bank account.

Access denied.

I tried again, slower this time. Same result.

My adversaries had gotten there first and added another layer of security. I couldn't get into Thomas Keene's account.

I closed it and moved on to Javier Morales.

Same lockout. Same added security.

I leaned back, careful of my ribs, and nodded once.

They'd moved fast.

Not panic. Damage control.

There was no doubt in my mind that all of the accounts of missing tenants at The Ashford had been shut down. No more AESS payments would be made to them. No more money would be diverted into the corporate accounts at North Meridian Private Bank.

The Ashford accounts were probably a rounding error to them.

I wasn't.

I'd need to be very careful going forward.

I pivoted.

Decided to follow the one lead I still had.

Thomas Kline.

I went to the Maricopa County Assessor's site. Property search. Name field.

I entered his name.

The result came back clean and immediate.

Residential.

East Monterosa Street.

Arcadia Lite.

I didn't need a map. I knew the neighborhood—the streets, the houses, the price range. Close enough to look legitimate. Tight enough to require explanation.

I did the math without writing it down.

Estimated his salary.

Mortgage.

Taxes.

Time on the job.

Living in the Arcadia Lite section of town would be a stretch for Thomas Kline.

That told me something else, too.

Thomas Kline wasn't the architect. He was a field operator. A paid one.

I needed to find out who was paying him.

I closed the laptop and rested my head back for a moment, eyes shut, letting the pressure settle and shift.

I knew what I would do next.

I just needed to be steady enough to do it—and not think too hard about the consequences.

# CHAPTER 26

I TOOK A TAXI.

Not because it was faster. Because the digital trail it left was harder to follow than an Uber ride.

The driver didn't ask questions. I gave him the address, leaned back carefully, and let the city slide past the window while my ribs complained in low, steady increments. The gun club sat north and east of where I'd started—far enough to matter, close enough to feel intentional.

I watched the streets anyway. Old habit.

When we pulled into the lot, I paid, stepped out, and waited a second before moving, letting the dizziness fade. The building hadn't changed since the last time I'd been there. Clean. Neutral. Purpose-built. A place where decisions were made without drama.

Inside, the air smelled faintly of oil and rubber. The counter staff looked up, assessed, moved on. No curiosity. No interest. That suited me.

I told them what I was there for.

There was no debate. No browsing. No nostalgia.

Glock 19.

Compact enough to carry. Large enough to matter. Familiar weight. Familiar lines. Not a statement—just the right tool.

Paperwork followed. ID checked. Forms signed. The background check cleared without ceremony.

Just yesterday, I'd killed a man with the same kind of gun. It had been self-defense. At least, that was my determination.

No court had ruled on it yet. Probably never would.

That was enough.

I felt the pressure behind my eyes tighten while I waited, then ease again.

When the case was set in front of me, I opened it, checked the chamber, the slide, the magazine. Everything where it should be.

I considered taking the gun to the range.

I could hear it through the wall—sharp reports, controlled rhythm. Muscle memory tugged at me. It would have been easy to step through the door, load, fire, remind my hands what they already knew.

But my shoulder had stiffened while I stood there. My ribs didn't like the idea of recoil yet. Neither did my head.

Today wasn't about proving anything.

I decided against the range, loaded the gun, and slipped it into the holster. Tested the draw once, slowly. No rush. No wasted movement.

The weight settled against my hip, familiar enough to feel like it belonged there again.

Restored. Not activated.

I called for another taxi from the desk and stepped outside.

The ride back felt different.

Not safer. Just narrower. Fewer unknowns. Fewer bad options.

As the taxi merged into traffic, I rested my head back and closed my eyes for a moment, letting the engine's vibration blur the edges of the ache.

I hoped I wouldn't need the gun.

I'd learned better than to count on hope.

I stayed in my apartment until the light outside my windows thinned and broke apart.

Dusk came first, then the deeper blue that softened edges and stretched shadows. By the time the streetlights came on, my ribs had loosened enough that I could move without negotiating every step.

That was the window I wanted.

I left on foot, locking the door behind me, and walked to the main road where taxis still cruised without purpose. The driver didn't ask where I'd been or why I wasn't driving myself. I gave him an address a few blocks short of the one I actually wanted and leaned back, watching the city darken.

The taxi stopped where I wanted it to.

I paid in cash, waited until the car pulled away, then started walking. The neighborhood was settling into evening—the quiet transition where people were still outside but no longer paying attention. Porch lights flicked on. A dog barked once and then stopped. Somewhere, a television laughed.

My ribs tightened as I walked, not enough to slow me down, just enough to keep me honest. I adjusted my pace and kept going.

The house was exactly where the map said it would be.

Single-story. Stucco. A yard that had been landscaped carefully once and then maintained just enough to keep it from sliding backward. The lights were on inside. Warm. Ordinary.

I didn't stop. First pass only.

I crossed the street, glanced once, then kept moving until I reached the corner. No cars idling. No one watching from a window. No obvious cameras. I circled the block and came back slower this time.

Dinner was in progress.

I could see it through the kitchen window as I passed—movement, shadows, the clink of something set down too hard. A woman at the counter. Two children at the table. A routine unfolding the same way it had a hundred times before.

This wasn't reconnaissance for sentiment. It was context.

I waited until the street quieted a little more, then slipped between houses and into the darkness along the back fence. The ground was dry. Gravel crunching underfoot, but softly. I stayed still when a light flicked on inside, then moved again when it went off.

The backyard was small. Functional. A grill. A couple of plastic chairs. No motion lights. No cameras that I could see.

I stayed back, close to the fence, where the shadows held.

The sliding door opened.

Thomas Kline stepped out onto the patio alone. He wore a dress shirt with the sleeves rolled up and the collar open a few buttons. He reached into his pocket, pulled out a cigarette, and lit it with the kind of practiced economy that comes from repetition.

I watched the smoke curl upward and disappear.

Smoker.

That mattered.

Not tonight—but soon.

He stood there for less than five minutes, scrolling on his phone with one hand, the cigarette burning down between his fingers. No urgency. No tension. A man who still believed his day had ended the way it was supposed to, in spite of my intrusion yesterday.

The temptation came fast.

I could step forward. Say his name. Watch his face change. I had the position. The darkness. The leverage.

I felt the thought settle, heavy and insistent.

And then I let it go.

This wasn't the place. And it wasn't the way.

Confronting him here would cost more than it gained. It would be illegal. Messy. Permanent. And it would teach him the wrong lesson—that he needed to protect his home.

What I needed was to understand his habits. His gaps. Where he thought he was safe.

He finished the cigarette, stubbed it out on the edge of the grill, and went back inside without looking around.

I stayed where I was for another thirty seconds. Then I moved.

Clean exit. No sound. No trace.

By the time I reached the sidewalk again, the street had gone quiet. The house behind me looked no different than it had before.

But I knew where he lived.

And I knew he stepped outside to smoke when he thought no one was watching.

That would be enough—for now.

# CHAPTER 27

MARA NOTICED THE bruises before she noticed anything else.

"You look like hell," she said quietly, not unkindly. "What happened?"

"Long story," I said. "Not one we should tell in here."

Her eyes flicked toward the hallway, then back to me. "You want coffee?"

"Sure, but not here."

That got her attention.

We waited until the morning rush thinned—deliveries logged, complaints fielded, the building settling into its daily rhythm. Then we stepped outside together, went to the coffee shop across the street.

I felt it in my ribs when I sat down, breathed too deeply and adjusted without thinking about it.

Mara noticed that too.

"You're hurt," she said.

"I'm fine," I said. Then, after a beat, "But you're not."

She frowned. "What does that mean?"

"It means I don't know who you're really working for," I said. "And neither do you."

She stopped walking.

"I work for the Westbridges," she said automatically. "Everyone here does."

I shook my head. "Are you saying the Westbridges are making all the decisions about what goes on in this building?"

That one stopped her. I could see the answer forming and then dying at the same time. She just needed a nudge.

The waitress came over, and we ordered coffee.

I took mine black.

Mara customized hers.

She studied my face. The bruises helped. I hadn't planned that, but I wasn't going to waste it.

"People connected to this place are getting hurt," I said. "Or worse. And I think it's only a matter of time before someone decides you know too much."

Her jaw tightened. "You don't know that."

"I know what happened to Gareth Cole."

She looked away.

"Everyone knows Gareth left," she said. "He—"

"He didn't leave," I said. "And you know it."

That landed.

She crossed her arms, a small, protective gesture. "You don't have proof."

"No," I said. "But I have patterns. And I know how this ends for people who ask the wrong questions, or get in the way without even meaning to."

She was quiet for a long moment.

She looked at me again. Really looked.

"It's not the Westbridges," she said.

The words came out flat. Certain.

I felt the shift immediately—the subtle realignment that happens when someone finally decides to tell the truth instead of the version they've been repeating to themselves.

"Okay," I said. "Then tell me who."

She hesitated.

Whatever she was about to say, it scared her.

"I can't," she said finally. "Not now. We need to get back."

"That's fine," I said. "You don't have to tell me now. And you're right, we should get back."

I could see that she was afraid. But not of me.

She let out a breath she'd been holding. "You're not going to report me, are you?"

"For what?" I asked. "Doing your job?"

She gave a short, humorless laugh. "That's what Gareth said."

I didn't respond to that.

We left the coffee shop and went back to The Ashford together. To anyone watching, it probably looked like two coworkers just finishing a break.

But something had shifted between us.

In the right direction.

Walker and Reyes came into the office in the early afternoon. I led them back into my office. Closed the door behind us. They sat in the two seats in front of my desk and started the interview.

I assumed they already knew about AESS.

Walker didn't lead with it. He let the conversation settle first—routine questions, neutral tone, the kind of opening that pretends it's about paperwork. Reyes was quiet, watching me instead of his notebook.

Then Walker said, "You were at AESS the morning of the incident."

Not a question.

"We know it was shortly before the vehicular assault," he added. "We're trying to understand why."

I didn't rush to answer. I'd learned not to respond to the frame someone else wanted. But I also knew the time had come to give them something.

"If you're focused on AESS," I said, "you're missing the real problem."

That got both of them.

Walker paused. Reyes shifted, attention sharpening.

"This isn't about redirected payments," I continued. "Or administrative errors. Or a state agency losing track of files. People are missing. Tenants from this very building just never came home one day."

Walker stopped writing.

I laid out what I could—timelines, gaps, patterns. No names. No explanations of how I knew what I knew. Just enough to move the center of gravity.

"This is far more than a fraud case," I said. "It's a missing persons problem."

The room changed.

The questions slowed. Names replaced numbers. Timelines replaced bank statements. Who was last seen where? Who noticed first? Who didn't ask questions and why?

Then Walker asked, "What about your assistant? She's been here a long time."

I answered without hesitation.

"Her former boss told her he'd taken care of everything," I said. "Including notifying the police. His name was Gareth Cole."

Walker and Reyes exchanged a look.

"We'll need to speak with her," Walker said.

No accusation. Just inevitability.

I could feel the clock tightening.

Inside, something else clicked into place. The Westbridges were insulated by design. Everything filtered downward—superintendents, administrators, maintenance personnel. No direct orders. No signatures. Plausible deniability engineered into the structure.

AESS wasn't the crime. It was the mechanism.

Walker closed his folder, then opened it again. "We need to see the apartments," he said. "All of them. The missing tenants. And Cole's."

He didn't ask for permission.

"Of course," I said. "I'll get you access."

That was the moment I knew I was out of time.

If Walker was here, others would follow. If they were walking apartments, someone would want to follow the money. Someone always did. And once the police were fully engaged, AESS wouldn't stay peripheral for long.

Jonathan Kline wouldn't wait around for that.

I stood and walked them past Mara, then left them outside the office and went back in. Closed the door behind me.

Mara looked up when I came in. She took in my

face, the stiffness in my movement, and straightened immediately.

"They're going to need access to the missing tenants' apartments," I said quietly. "All of them. Including Gareth Cole's."

Her jaw tightened. She didn't argue.

"I have a doctor's appointment," I added. It wasn't a lie anyone would question. "I won't be here. They'll need you."

I handed her the master key.

She hesitated just long enough for doubt to flicker.

I met her eyes.

"You're going to be okay," I said, keeping my voice low. "You did nothing wrong. You followed Gareth's orders. Right?"

Mara swallowed, then nodded once.

"Right," she said.

I squeezed her hand briefly and stepped back into the hall, already moving.

Walker and Reyes were waiting outside. They weren't happy that I'd gone back in and briefed Mara.

"I asked my assistant to let you in," I said. "I've got a doctor's appointment."

Walker studied me for a second, then nodded.

As I turned away, I felt the pressure fully now—not fear, exactly, but urgency with teeth.

The police were about to open doors that had been kept closed for a long time.

And I had one last chance to reach Thomas Kline before that happened.

# CHAPTER 28

I NEEDED TO MOVE fast.

Lingering would cost more than it gained.

I stepped out into the afternoon sun and flagged a taxi without looking back.

"Arizona Emergency Support Services," I said when the door shut.

The driver nodded, entered the name into his GPS, and pulled away from the curb.

The city slid past the window in clean, familiar lines. Traffic lights. Cross streets. People moving through their day without any sense of the clock that had just started ticking. I sat still, my shooting hand resting at my side, the weight at my hip a reminder rather than a threat.

My ribs protested when we hit a shallow dip in the road. Not enough to matter. Just enough to register.

I was steady.

Not healed.

That mattered too, but not right now.

We reached the AESS complex in under fifteen minutes. I paid the driver in cash and stepped out before he could ask if I wanted change. I was out near the edge of the parking lot, far enough away that no one would remember the drop-off later.

The building was set far enough back from the road that it insulated itself from casual attention, which made it easier to watch without being watched.

I didn't go inside.

Instead, I walked the perimeter.

Slow. Casual. Like someone killing time before an appointment.

I clocked the exits first. Two obvious, one service door tucked around the side. Cameras were visible, but not aggressive—positioned to deter vandalism, not track movement. As I walked closer to the building, reflections in the tinted glass showed me fragments of myself as I passed: blazer, slacks, dark hair pulled back, the faint discoloration along my cheekbone that no amount of lighting could hide.

I chose a bench near the side of the building, close to a concrete butt can that had seen better days. Not an official smoking area. Just a place smokers had claimed over time.

I sat.

No phone out. No visible impatience.

The sun sat high, the light flat and revealing. Two o'clock, give or take. That was the rhythm here—lunch breaks ending, afternoon settling in. People slipping out for cigarettes under the pretense of needing air.

I waited.

The first group came out together. Three men, one woman. Lanyards loose, conversations half-finished.

They clustered near the wall, laughed at something small, lit up with the easy efficiency of people who'd done this a hundred times before.

I didn't move.

They finished, crushed their cigarettes, and went back inside.

A few minutes passed.

Then Thomas Kline came out alone.

He didn't look around the way someone hiding something did. He walked with the mild impatience of a man who believed he was entitled to this break. He passed the butt can at first, then doubled back, positioning himself farther down the wall, angled slightly away from the entrance.

Separate, but not suspicious.

He lit his cigarette and took a long first drag, shoulders dropping as the nicotine hit.

That told me a lot.

He was feeling stress today that he hadn't been feeling yesterday.

I waited one more beat.

Then I stood.

I didn't hurry. I didn't hesitate. I closed the distance at a normal pace and stopped beside him, far enough not to crowd him, close enough that he couldn't pretend I wasn't there.

I let him see my face.

The bruises. The cuts. The evidence that something had already gone wrong.

"Hello, Mr. Kline," I said.

Low. Even.

He startled despite himself. Not a flinch—just a quick tightening, the cigarette pausing halfway to his mouth. He recognized me.

"What are you doing here?" he said immediately.

"I'm talking to you."

He exhaled smoke, slow and controlled. His eyes flicked to the building, then back to me.

"You should leave," he said. "This isn't appropriate."

I watched his hand. Steady. No shake. He wasn't panicking yet.

"Police are opening apartments at The Ashford right now," I said. "Including Gareth Cole's."

That did it.

His jaw set. The cigarette burned untouched between his fingers.

"You don't know what you're talking about," he said. "I process files. I don't make decisions."

"I know what you process," I said. "And I know what happens after."

He laughed once. Short. Defensive.

"You think you're the first person to walk in here with a theory?" he said. "This is a state agency. Everything we do is documented."

"Yes," I said. "And people still disappear."

That landed differently.

He took another drag, longer this time, buying himself a second. I let him have it.

"The police are going to come here," I said. "Soon. Not today. Not loudly. But they will."

"You don't scare me," he said, too quickly.

"I'm not trying to."

I turned slightly so he could see the building reflected in the glass. The quiet. The normalcy.

"The police are the least of your problems," I said. "You work for people who don't leave witnesses behind. They leave gaps."

His mouth tightened.

"You should be very worried about what happens when you stop being useful," I went on. "Because when that happens, you don't get a warning. You get erased. Same as the tenants."

He swallowed.

"And your family," I added, then stopped myself, as if reconsidering. "I don't know what they do with families. I just know they don't like loose ends."

That was the moment.

Not fear. Calculation.

He looked at me fully now, seeing past the bruises, weighing what it would cost to keep pretending.

"What do you want?" he asked.

"To catch them," I said. "It could help you if I do."

"You don't know who you're dealing with."

"I do," I said. "I've seen what's left behind when they're done."

He pressed his lips together, cigarette forgotten, smoke curling up between us.

Finally, he nodded once.

"Okay," he said. "But I don't know their names."

"I'm not asking for names," I said.

That surprised him.

I shifted—not closer, not farther. Just enough to change the shape of the conversation.

"How do they contact you?" I asked.

He blinked. Reset.

"Text," he said. "Always text."

"From the same number?"

"No." He shook his head. "Different every time."

"What do they send?"

"An address," he said. "Sometimes with a unit number. Never explanations."

"Never names?"

"Never names."

That told me everything I needed to know about the structure. Cells. Compartmentalization. Disposable operators.

"They reached out recently, didn't they?" I said.

He hesitated.

"Yes."

"This morning?"

"Yes."

"For a meeting."

He nodded.

"I'm not going," he said. "I'm leaving. Tonight. Family first."

That wasn't panic. That was a man who'd seen enough endings to recognize the pattern.

"You should turn yourself in," I said. "Make a deal."

He shook his head immediately.

"Deals collapse," he said. "The protection fails. People like me don't get saved."

I didn't argue.

He wasn't wrong.

"Give me the address," I said.

He looked at me, really looked this time.

"I'm not asking you to go," I said quietly. "I'm not asking you to stay. I'm asking for a chance."

He exhaled, reached into his pocket, and pulled out his phone.

He held it where I could see the screen. A single message. An address.

I took out my phone and photographed it.

"When do they expect you?" I asked.

"Midnight," he said. "Always."

That landed hard.

I stepped back.

"Good luck," I said.

He didn't respond.

I walked away without looking back, the address burned into my mind, the clock already counting down.

Midnight.

Whatever was coming would happen with or without him.

And now I'd be there.

# CHAPTER 29

I DIDN'T TURN ON the lights yet.

The sun had already gone down, but there was still enough ambient glow from the street that I didn't need it. The apartment felt neutral—neither day nor night. A place between.

Walker's card was on the kitchen counter where I'd left it.

I picked it up, looked at it once, and dialed.

He answered after a couple of rings.

"Hi, Kate," he said. "What can I do for you?"

"I've got something," I said. "Not enough yet. But close."

He didn't rush me.

"Okay," he said. "Tell me what you know."

"There's a meeting," I said. "Tonight. Midnight."

A brief pause. Not surprise. Just recalibration.

"Where?"

"I'm not going to give you the address yet."

"All right."

That was it. No challenge. No pushback.

“I need to confirm it first,” I said. “I want to make sure it’s real.”

“Fair,” he said. “How are you planning to do that?”

“I’m going to watch it,” I said. “See who shows up. How many. What kind of place it is.”

“And then?”

“If it’s nothing, you won’t hear from me,” I said. “If it’s something, I’ll call you and give you the address.”

Another pause. Shorter this time.

“You want me ready,” he said.

“Yes.”

“I can do that,” he said. “Quietly.”

“That’s what I’m asking for.”

“Are you going alone?”

“Yes.”

“Armed?”

“Yes.”

He didn’t comment on that.

“Are you safe right now?” he asked.

I took a moment before answering. Not because I was unsure, but because the question deserved a considered response.

“Yes,” I said. “For now.”

“All right,” he said. “Call me as soon as you know what you’re looking at.”

“I will.”

“And Kate?”

“Yes.”

“Don’t take risks you can’t walk away from.”

“I won’t.”

That wasn't a promise. It was what I believed at the time.

We hung up.

I set the phone back on the counter and stood there for a moment, listening to the faint sounds of traffic outside. Somewhere down the block, a car door closed. Voices drifted, then faded.

Walker wouldn't move yet. That was the point. But he'd be on it. Thinking. Quietly lining things up down at PPD headquarters.

I checked the time.

Early evening. Still hours to go.

I went to the hall closet and pulled down a small backpack I hadn't used in a while. From the front pocket, I took out the camera I'd carried when I was still a detective, and later, during fieldwork at the AG's office.

I checked the settings, then slid it back into the pack. Compact, quiet, built for low light. Not something I'd trust my phone to do. I zipped the bag and slung it over my shoulder.

I went into the bedroom and pulled on dark jeans and a jacket I could shed if I needed to.

Midnight wasn't close.

But it was fixed.

And when it came, I hoped I wouldn't be the only one paying attention.

The taxi driver didn't ask questions.

I gave the address Kline had shown me and watched the driver enter it into his GPS without comment. We pulled away from the curb and headed west, the city thinning in stages rather than all at once.

Downtown light gave way to longer gaps between streetlamps. Businesses closed earlier out here. The sidewalks emptied faster. Night didn't arrive all at once—it seeped in, replacing daytime patterns with something looser and less predictable. It wasn't a coincidence that most of the crime in Phoenix took place on this side of town.

I stayed quiet and watched reflections in the glass.

Cars moved differently now. Fewer signals. More rolling stops. People driving with purpose instead of routine. The farther west we went, the less anyone seemed to expect to be noticed.

That wasn't paranoia. It was habit.

The driver slowed as we approached the address.

"Want me to pull up front?" he asked.

"No," I said. "Just up here's fine."

He stopped a block short. I paid in cash and stepped out before he could ask anything else.

The air was cooler than it had been earlier, the kind of dry January chill that didn't bite but didn't disappear either. I waited until the taxi pulled away before I started walking.

The building came into view gradually, not announced by signage or lighting, just present.

Low-slung. Rectangular. Set back from the street with a shallow lot in front and nothing decorative to draw the eye. A few exterior lights were on—not bright, not dark. Enough to function. Not enough to stand out.

No name that mattered.

No branding.

If you weren't looking for it, you'd pass by without registering it at all.

That told me what I needed to know.

This place didn't advertise. It didn't invite. It survived by being overlooked.

I crossed the street and kept walking past it, letting myself take it in without stopping. Windows were few and high. No obvious activity inside, but not dead either. The lights that were on suggested occupancy without revealing purpose.

Corporate-adjacent. Industrial enough to justify late hours. Generic enough to blend into a hundred other blocks like it.

I reached the corner and turned, circling back on the opposite side.

Diagonally across from the building was a small park—more of a leftover strip of city planning than a destination. A concrete restroom sat near the top of a slight incline, windowless and squat, its exterior scarred with old graffiti that had long since been painted over.

I walked to it without hesitation and leaned against the side wall, positioning myself where I could see the building clearly without being silhouetted by the streetlights.

From here, I had elevation, cover, and a clean line of sight. I'd be able to see the faces of any people who arrived as they walked into the building.

But they wouldn't see me.

I checked my watch.

Still early.

I settled in and waited.

At eleven-thirty, the first car arrived.

It didn't slow much as it pulled up to the curb. No hazard lights. No hesitation. Just a smooth stop, close enough that the passenger didn't have to step off the pavement.

The man got out alone.

Mid-forties, maybe older. Dark coat, nothing distinctive about it. The kind of clothing meant to survive weather and cameras without comment. He didn't look around when the car pulled away. He didn't need to.

I raised the camera and brought the lens to my eye.

I took three shots as he crossed the sidewalk. One head-on. One profile. One as he reached the door. There was no sound as the camera did its job. By design.

He didn't knock.

He pulled out a key and unlocked it.

That mattered.

It meant he was in charge of this meeting.

The door opened just long enough for him to step inside before it closed again, leaving the building exactly as it had been before — blank, unremarkable, uninviting.

I checked the time.

Eleven thirty-two.

The next arrival came six minutes later.

Another car. Different make. Different driver. Same pattern. Stop, drop, gone.

This man was younger. Thirties. Cleaner haircut. He hesitated just long enough at the curb to suggest uncertainty, then crossed to the door without looking back.

I photographed him too.

Clear shots. Face, posture, gait.

He didn't knock either.

The door opened immediately.

By eleven forty-five, six men had gone in, but more kept coming.

No two arrived together. No one lingered. No one spoke outside. The cars never waited long enough to be useful — gone before I could even consider a plate.

That wasn't a failure.

It was the point.

I documented each arrival carefully, the camera steady in my hands. Faces first. Then the moment each one reached the door. Then the empty street after the car left.

No vehicles accumulated in the lot.

No shared transport.

No visible connections.

Just men arriving one by one, disappearing inside, and leaving nothing behind.

Except themselves.

One person who hadn't arrived was Thomas Kline. Probably long gone by now, with his confused family in tow. But he'd been true to his word. The meeting was coming down at midnight.

At eleven fifty-three, the last arrival stepped out of a rideshare I recognized without needing to check my notes.

Ray Donnelly.

He looked as he always did — competent, forgettable, the kind of man you'd trust to handle a problem without ever asking how he'd done it. His coat was lighter than the others', his posture looser. He paused at the curb for half a second, like someone orienting himself.

Then he walked toward the door.

I took the photos.

Clear. Clean. No blur.

The door opened for him before he reached it.

That was when it clicked fully into place.

This wasn't a meeting called in response to pressure.

It wasn't improvisation.

These people met regularly. Just not on a pre-determined schedule or at the same place.

A room full of men who didn't drive themselves and didn't leave evidence behind — except the fact that they existed.

I lowered the camera and checked the time.

Eleven fifty-eight.

I had the photos, but they were just insurance in case the men inside got away.

I slipped the camera into the backpack and pulled out my phone.

I stayed where I was.

The building was still in view. Lights unchanged. No movement at the door. Whatever was happening inside was meant to stay there.

I dialed Walker's number.

He answered on the second ring.

"Walker."

"It's real," I said.

No response. No questions. Just listening.

"Multiple arrivals," I said. "All drop-offs. No cars left behind. One of them is the maintenance man from The Ashford. You know what that means."

"I do," he said. "How many?"

"At least a dozen people," I said. "They're inside now."

A short pause.

"Are you safe?" he asked.

"So far."

Another beat.

"What's the address?" he asked.

I gave it to him.

"Don't come in hot," I said.

"Understood," he said.

I ended the call and slipped the phone back into my pocket.

Nothing changed.

The building remained quiet. No doors opening. No one leaving. Whatever had brought them here was still in progress.

I kept watching.

From where I stood, the building looked exactly as it had when I arrived.

Lights on.

Doors closed.

People inside.

Business continuing.

This wasn't a one-off meeting.

It wasn't just The Ashford.

It was a system that moved people quietly and gave others access where it mattered.

I no longer wondered if this was real—only how far it went.

I stayed put and waited for Walker's team to arrive.

# CHAPTER 30

THE CONCRETE RESTROOM wall was cool against my shoulder as I leaned against it, the hill sloping gently away beneath my feet. From here, I had the parking lot, the front of the building, and the dark ribbon of road feeding into it. Nothing moved. The lights inside the building hadn't changed.

I checked the time again without really meaning to.

Twelve-nineteen.

The camera sat zipped inside the backpack at my feet, weightless now. Insurance. Useful later, maybe. But photos weren't the main objective. The men inside were still the point.

I focused on the road.

The first set of headlights appeared, slowly and deliberately approaching the building. They didn't pull up to the curb. They eased in, angled slightly across the lot the way patrol cars do when they expect to leave fast.

Marked unit.

Two officers stepped out, uniforms dark against the

lot lights. No rush. No lights. No sirens. Just controlled movement, practiced enough to look casual.

My pulse picked up anyway.

The second unit arrived less than a minute later and took the opposite angle, creating a shallow V that pointed directly at the building. Doors opened. More uniforms. A brief exchange I couldn't hear but recognized instantly—quick, economical, all business.

Then the unmarked car came in behind them.

Walker was driving. Reyes in the passenger seat.

They didn't park with the others. They stopped just outside the light spill, far enough back to see everything without being seen themselves. Walker got out, scanned the building once, then the lot, then the hill where I stood—too far away for him to see me, but close enough that I felt the instinctive tightening anyway.

This was it.

This was the moment where things stopped being theoretical.

The officers spread out, each one moving with a purpose that didn't need to be discussed. Two took the sides of the building, shadows sliding along the wall. One stayed near the vehicles, hand on the radio. Another positioned himself near the edge of the lot, eyes on the road.

Containment.

They weren't treating this like a hostage situation. No shouting. Weapons were out, but down at their side. This was what it looked like when cops believed something was wrong—but didn't yet know how wrong.

Walker and Reyes stayed back, watching.

Reyes said something to him, low, and Walker nodded once.

I leaned slightly forward without meaning to, the way you do when the end of a story is approaching, and you can feel it before it arrives.

They moved as a group toward the entrance.

No one ran. No one hesitated.

The building seemed to absorb them as they crossed the last stretch of open pavement, the light flattening them into silhouettes. For a brief second, I had the irrational thought that the door might simply open for them the way it had for the others.

It didn't.

One of the uniforms reached for the handle and tested it.

Nothing.

A quick knock. Firm. Official.

No response.

I held my breath without realizing it.

There was a pause—not long, but long enough to matter. Long enough for Walker to step forward, for Reyes to shift his stance, for the choice to settle.

Then they went for the door.

They didn't smash the glass. They went for the seam, a flat steel bar wedged into the slit where the door met the frame, where the building admitted it could be forced. The sound carried even up the hill—a sharp, controlled crack that echoed once and then died.

The door gave way.

The first two uniforms went in immediately, bodies

disappearing into the rectangle of light. Then another. Then Reyes.

Walker waited a beat longer than the rest.

He looked at the lot once more, then the road, then stepped inside and pulled the door after him.

The building closed around them.

I exhaled slowly.

This was the part where the story usually broke one way or the other.

If they were inside—if the men were still there—this would turn fast. Voices. Movement. Commands. The unmistakable shape of something coming undone.

If not—

I didn't finish the thought.

Minutes passed.

The lights inside stayed on. No flicker. No shadows racing across the windows. No raised voices, no crashes, no sudden violence spilling outward.

I checked the time again.

Twelve twenty-eight.

Too long.

My excitement—the sharp, almost electric certainty that they were finally going to catch these people—began to thin, stretched out by time and silence until it changed shape.

I'd felt this before.

This was what it felt like when a room was supposed to be full and wasn't.

When you were waiting for a sound that never came.

The night pressed back in around me. A breeze moved through the trees behind the restroom. Somewhere far off, a siren wailed, unrelated and fading. A car passed on a cross street I couldn't see.

Still nothing from the building.

Twelve thirty-four.

I shifted my weight, careful not to step out of the shadows. My eyes never left the door.

This wasn't a sweep. This wasn't a negotiation. This was taking too long for something that should have resolved already—one way or the other.

The door opened.

One uniform stepped out.

He didn't have anyone with him.

His shoulders were wrong. Too loose. No tension, no urgency. He stopped just outside the doorway and looked back in, waiting.

Another officer followed.

Then another.

Then Reyes.

No cuffs. No hands raised. No one being guided or pushed or restrained.

The lot remained empty.

Walker came out last.

He stood just outside the doorway and looked at the ground for a moment, then up at the building, as if trying to reconcile what it was supposed to contain with what it had given him instead.

Nothing.

Reyes said something I couldn't hear. Walker shook his head once.

Then he pulled out his phone and dialed.

Mine vibrated.

I didn't look at the screen. I already knew.

I answered on the first ring.

"What happened?" I said.

There was a pause on the other end. Not long. Just enough to tell me he was choosing his words—and failing.

"That's my question," Walker said. "Where the fuck are these people?"

I stayed where I was, the building still in my line of sight, its lights unchanged, its doors closed again.

Whoever had been inside had already moved on.

# CHAPTER 31

I WAITED UNTIL WALKER stepped back into the light before I moved.

From the hill, I could see the way he stood—hands at his sides, shoulders squared, not rushed. That told me more than the empty parking lot ever could. Whatever they'd found inside, it wasn't enough.

I came down the path slowly, staying out of sight until I reached the edge of the lot. The building looked unchanged from here. Same lights. Same doors. Same quiet.

Walker spotted me before I reached him. His expression didn't shift—no surprise, no irritation—but his eyes sharpened slightly, the way they do when a piece clicks into place.

"You shouldn't have been up there," he said.

"I told you I was close," I said. "I didn't move."

He nodded once. That was the end of it.

Inside, officers were already peeling away, one by one. No urgency. No noise. Radios murmured. Doors opened and closed. It had the loose, anticlimactic feel of a call that didn't pay off.

Reyes stood near the entrance, speaking quietly to one of the uniforms. When he saw me, he broke off and came over.

"You were right," he said.

About what? I didn't ask. I already knew the answer.

Walker gestured toward the door. "You want to see?"

"I do."

We stepped inside. Followed a corridor to a conference room in the interior of the building.

The air was warm—not hot, just lived-in. Stale coffee. A faint chemical note I couldn't place at first. Cleaner, maybe. Something wiped down too quickly.

The room itself was almost bare. A long table. Folding chairs stacked against the wall. A whiteboard with nothing on it but faint smudges where something had been erased. The floor was clean. Too clean.

Walker moved through the space slowly, narrating without drama.

"They were here," he said. "Recently."

"How recently?" I asked.

"Tonight," Reyes said. "Like you said."

There were paper cups in a trash bag near the door. Still damp inside. No fingerprints worth anything. No trash left behind that mattered.

"They didn't panic," Walker said. "They cleared out. On foot. Went out the proverbial back door."

I walked the perimeter, not touching anything. The chairs had been stacked deliberately, not shoved aside. Whoever left had taken the time to restore order.

"They knew exactly how long they had," I said.

Walker didn't argue.

"No electronics," Reyes added. "No laptops. No phones. Nothing to pull data from."

"And no people," Walker said. "Which makes it complicated."

"Complicated how?" I asked.

Reyes answered. "No probable cause to chase. No IDs. No vehicles tied to the scene. By the time we realized what we were dealing with, they were already gone."

"Dispersed," I said.

Walker nodded. "That's the word."

I stopped near the whiteboard, studying the ghost of whatever had been there before. Someone had erased it thoroughly—but not angrily. No streaks. No scratches. Just absence.

"They didn't leave anything by accident," I said.

"No," Walker agreed. "They didn't."

I took the camera from my backpack and held it out. "I have faces." Scrolled through a few of them so he could see.

Walker looked at it, then at me. "We'll need that."

"I'll email them to you when I get home," I said.

A beat.

"Do that," he said.

I slipped the camera back into the bag.

"They weren't surprised," I said.

Walker turned to face me fully.

"By the arrival," I added. "They expected it. Or they were prepared for it."

Reyes looked between us but didn't speak.

Walker exhaled slowly through his nose. "We're going to have to assume that."

"Which means—" I started.

"—someone talked," Walker finished.

I didn't say the word. Neither did he.

Walker looked around the room one last time, then back at me. "This isn't over," he said.

"No," I agreed. "It just moved."

He held my gaze for a moment longer than necessary, then nodded toward the door.

"Let's step outside."

Reyes slowed as we reached the doorway.

"I've got to take this," he said, already stepping away, one hand lifting his phone from his pocket.

Walker didn't look back. He just nodded and kept walking.

Walker stayed just outside the building, one hand braced against the doorframe, looking back in as if the room might still explain itself if he gave it enough time.

It didn't.

"This isn't standard anymore," he said finally.

He didn't raise his voice. He didn't lower it either. The words landed where they landed.

"Standard how?" I asked.

He turned to face me. "This wasn't a one-off meeting. It wasn't opportunistic. Whatever they're doing, it's organized."

I nodded. That much had already been clear.

"And organized things like this," he continued, "don't usually stay inside one city. Or one department. Or one clean line of authority."

He didn't say anything else. He didn't have to.

Walker shifted his weight, the way he did when he was thinking several steps ahead and not liking where they led. "I'm not saying we stop. I'm saying we adjust."

I let that sit between us for a moment before he went on.

"How did you know to be here tonight?" he asked.

The question wasn't accusatory. It was careful. He wasn't looking for a confession. He was assessing a variable.

"I got a tip," I said.

"I know that," he said. "I want to know who it was."

I didn't answer right away.

"Thomas Kline," I said finally. "AESS. He's the one who was moving the money."

Walker's eyes narrowed slightly. Not surprise. Recognition.

"He told me because he knew he was out of time," I said. "I think he thought that whatever I could do here might slow them down. He was wrong. Now they know he was the rat because he didn't show up to the meeting. And we didn't catch them."

"Where is he now?" Walker asked.

"Running," I said. "With his family, if he was smart."

Walker looked past me, out into the lot. Empty now. Just asphalt and light.

"He should have come to us," said Walker.

"Maybe," I said. "I told him to, but he seemed to have less faith in the system than I do. But that doesn't mean we should abandon him, does it?"

"Of course not," said Walker. "We'll find him. Protect

him. We'll need his testimony if we ever catch anyone." He shook his head, frustrated.

I nodded, unconvinced that anyone could be protected from these people.

Walker took in a deep breath and let it out slowly, the way someone does when a calculation finishes, whether they like the result or not. "That many people," he said. "At one meeting. They're into this city deep."

"Yep," I said.

"And you put this together by yourself," he said. "No badge. No cover."

"I didn't have a choice."

"You did," he said. "You just didn't take the safe one."

That was the closest he came to saying I shouldn't have done this. It was also the closest he came to saying I did exactly what needed to be done.

He looked at me again, really looked this time.

"You're not a civilian tip anymore," he said. "You're a sensor."

I didn't correct him.

"And sensors," he went on, "get noticed."

"Yes," I said. "They do."

For a moment, neither of us spoke. The building loomed behind him, silent and ordinary, like it hadn't just swallowed a dozen men and given nothing back.

Walker broke first.

"I think I need to give this to the Feds," he said.

There it was.

I felt the words land, settle, rearrange the room.

"I was afraid you were going to say that," I said.

He studied my face. "Why?"

"Because it makes sense," I said. "And because it ends my role in this."

"That's not—"

"I know," I said. "But it will."

He frowned. "You just said we probably have a mole. This thing is big. It crosses jurisdictions. We're all targets now."

"You're right," I said. "We are all targets. More than you might believe."

His eyes locked onto mine, intense. Maybe even alarmed. I met his gaze and didn't look away.

"You should know something before you do this," I said. "I tried to give this same case to the Feds when I was still at the AG's office."

Walker went still.

"They fired me for it," I said. "Blacklisted me. Not even PPD would hire me back."

The silence that followed wasn't awkward. It was heavy. A realization settling into place.

Walker looked back at the building again, then at me.

"I didn't know that," he said.

"No," I said. "You wouldn't have."

He nodded slowly, once.

Then, very carefully, he said, "Thank you for telling me."

The night pressed in around us. The lot stayed empty. And somewhere, not far from here, the people who had cleared this room were already adjusting to the fact that this had almost gone wrong.

# CHAPTER 32

WALKER OFFERED ME a ride home like it was a foregone conclusion.

Not a question. Not a favor. Just a statement delivered with the quiet authority of someone who had already weighed the variables—time of night, distance, what we'd just walked away from—and decided there was no point pretending this was optional.

I didn't argue.

It was late. Later than I liked being out without a reason, and I'd already spent mine. The meeting. The empty building. The sense that something had slipped through our hands without ever being solid enough to grab. Pride was a luxury at that hour, and safety was not.

I slid into the back seat. Walker took the wheel. Reyes climbed in front, shotgun, moving with a little too much energy for someone who'd just stood through a failed raid.

The doors shut. The car rolled forward.

For a while, no one spoke.

The city had thinned out around us, the streets quieter than they had any right to be. Sodium lights pooled on the pavement and broke apart again as we passed through them, the rhythm steady, almost hypnotic. I watched it all through the glass, letting my body settle back into the seat, feeling the delayed fatigue begin to creep in now that the adrenaline had faded.

Walker kept his eyes on the road. Both hands on the wheel. He drove in a controlled, unshowy way, like he wasn't interested in proving anything to anyone.

The silence between us wasn't awkward. It wasn't avoidance, either. It was something closer to recognition. Walker and I both knew this wasn't the moment to dissect what had happened, or what hadn't. Whatever conclusions we were going to draw would land harder if we gave them a little air first.

Reyes didn't share that instinct.

He shifted in his seat, cleared his throat, then leaned into the quiet like it was something he needed to fill.

"So," he said, glancing back at me, then forward again, as if checking his angles. "You said there were, what—ten guys? Twelve?"

"Yeah," I said, and I didn't elaborate.

He nodded, then pressed on. "And none of them looked familiar up close?" I guess Walker hadn't told him that I recognized Ray Donnelly. Best to keep it that way.

"I wasn't up close."

"What about the way they moved?" he asked. "Anything stand out?"

I kept my voice even. "They were careful."

He took that as encouragement. "Yeah. That's what I thought too. Real organized. Like they'd done it before."

I let a beat pass. Long enough for the comment to sit there without being fed.

Walker didn't react. He didn't shut Reyes down, but he didn't look back either. Just kept driving, the car steady in its lane.

Reyes tried again.

"You think they'll come back?" he asked. "Same place, I mean. Or do you think this was a one-off?"

That was a stupid question, to get me talking. I didn't bite.

"No idea," I said. "That's for you and Walker to figure out."

It wasn't sharp. It wasn't defensive. Just a redirection, clean and simple.

Reyes glanced at Walker, waiting for him to pick it up.

Walker didn't.

The silence returned, heavier this time. More deliberate.

I watched Reyes in the reflection of the rearview mirror. The way he sat forward in his seat. The way his knee bounced once, then stilled, then started again. He had the look of someone whose thoughts were moving faster than the situation merited, scrambling for purchase.

Young, I thought. Not inexperienced—he knew his way around a crime scene, knew how to follow procedure—but young in the way that mattered. Eager. The kind of cop who wanted to be useful, wanted to belong in rooms like the one we'd just walked out of.

The kind of cop who talked when silence would have served him better.

The thought came uninvited, fully formed: people like him didn't need ideology to be compromised. They didn't need to believe in anything crooked or abstract. They just needed opportunity. A little money. A little validation. Someone telling them they were on the right side of something bigger than themselves.

I didn't name the thought. I didn't need to.

The rest of the drive passed with only small, unnecessary comments from Reyes—half-formed theories, questions that circled too close to strategy for someone who shouldn't need answers yet. I deflected when I had to. Let them die when I could.

When the car finally slowed and pulled in front of my building, I felt something in my chest tighten—not fear exactly, but awareness.

Reyes turned in his seat, smiling, easy, polite.

"Get some rest," he said. "Long night."

"Yeah," I said.

When I lugged my sore body out of the car, the cool air hit my face and pulled me a little more awake.

Walker met my eyes through the rolled-up window. The warning was clear.

*Be careful.*

I nodded.

He nodded once, then drove away, his taillights shrinking until they vanished at the end of the block.

I stood there longer than I needed to.

My address wasn't a secret anymore.

Inside, I dropped my bag on the table and went straight to the laptop, the motion automatic, muscle memory taking over before my thoughts could catch up.

Walker's card was still in my pocket. I pulled it out, set it beside the keyboard, and opened a new email.

I didn't waste words.

I linked the laptop to the camera and downloaded the photos—faces, arrivals, angles. I prepared an email to Walker, attaching the photos in the sequence I'd taken them. Then I flagged the man who'd arrived first. The one who'd unlocked the door without hesitation, without looking around, like the space already belonged to him.

He had the key.

He had the confidence.

Everyone else had followed his lead.

If there was a spine to that meeting—someone who controlled access, who set the tone—it was him.

I told Walker that. Plainly. No speculation, just pattern. Highest priority ID.

The photos were clear enough for him to run through every facial-recognition database he had access to. If that came up empty, the next step would be the FBI—to widen the net, tap systems far deeper and far more sophisticated than anything the locals had.

I wondered if he'd do it.

He'd been wary after I told him what happened when I tried to take this case to the FBI.

I hit send and closed the laptop.

For the first time since the evening began, I let myself breathe.

Not relief. Not calm. Just the sense that I'd done everything I could during this very long day.

Tomorrow, Walker would work on the photos.

I'd go after my one remaining hot lead—Ray Donnelly.

# CHAPTER 33

RAY DONNELLY DIDN'T give me the chance to interview him.

He was already waiting when I came in, the office caught in that early, suspended hour before the day officially began. Mara wasn't in yet—she never arrived before eight-thirty—and the lights over the reception desk were the only ones on. Everything else felt half-asleep, undecided, as if the building itself were hesitating.

Ray stood near Mara's desk, hands at his sides, jacket still on. He didn't pace. He didn't fidget. He looked like someone who had already finished the hardest part and was just there to collect the remains.

He extended his arm and handed me an envelope.

"I'm resigning," he said.

No preamble. No apology. Just the fact of it, delivered evenly, as if he were reading it off a checklist he'd memorized on the drive over.

I didn't open the envelope. I didn't need to. I looked at him instead, trying to decide how much time I had left.

"The police are going to want to talk to you," I said. "You know that."

Ray nodded once. Not in agreement. In acknowledgment.

"This is your chance," I went on. "If there's anything you want to explain, anything you want to put on the record—now is the moment."

He met my eyes. Really met them. There was no anger there. No defensiveness. No attempt to perform outrage or innocence.

Just resolve.

"I've got to go," he said. Then, after a beat, "Can I get my last check?"

That was the tell.

Not the resignation. Not the timing. The check.

He wasn't here to argue. He wasn't here to clear his name. He wasn't even here to stall. He was just trying to gather as much money as he could before running off to who knows where.

"I don't know where Mara keeps the checkbook," I said.

"It's right in that drawer where she keeps the master key," he said.

"Yeah," I said. "But I haven't been down to the bank to register my signature. Mara will be in soon. Can you wait? "

"I don't think so," he said.

I understood why, but I tried to keep him from leaving anyway.

"You should talk to Walker," I said. "He can arrange for you to be protected."

Ray shook his head once, small and final. "Wouldn't change anything."

That's when it clicked.

He wasn't afraid of the police.

He was afraid of what came after.

Ray pressed his lips together, nodded goodbye, and turned toward the door. No backward glance. No hesitation.

I stood there for a moment after the door closed, still holding the envelope in my hand.

Another door had shut.

And the pressure, instead of easing, tightened.

When Mara arrived, I told her about Ray and suggested we leave the office to talk.

Mara looked at me for a moment, searching my face. Then she nodded. "Sounds like a good idea."

We locked up the office and left. We didn't go far. Back to the coffee shop across the street. The place smelled like burnt espresso and cinnamon, same as it had the first time we'd come here. It was the kind of local haunt where no one hurried you and no one listened. We grabbed our coffee at the counter and slid into a booth at the back, vinyl cracked from years of use, our voices naturally lowering once we sat.

I didn't waste time.

"Ray was part of it," I said. "Whatever's been happening here—he was involved. He's gone now because the people he was working for aren't happy about how things have unfolded."

Mara stiffened, just slightly. She wrapped both hands around her mug and didn't drink. "I figured he was part of it," she said.

"I need your help," I said. "If there's anything you've seen, anything that didn't sit right—I need you to tell me now."

She was quiet for a long moment. When she finally spoke, her voice was steady, but something underneath it had shifted.

"The Westbridges sold their property management business," she said. "Two years ago."

The words landed cleanly. Too cleanly.

I nodded once. "That's when Ray was hired."

"And Gareth Cole?"

Mara's mouth tightened. "Right around then."

I let the silence sit between us before asking the next question. "Who bought it?"

"Obsidian Venture Capital."

I took the notebook from my bag and wrote it down.

"Did you meet anyone from Obsidian?" I asked.

Mara thought about it. "One man. Older. British. Polite in a way that felt practiced."

"Did he work for them?" I asked.

"I don't know," she said. "He didn't act like staff. But he didn't act like ownership, either. He was very friendly. He used the penthouse when he came through. Everyone referred to him as Mr. Pembroke."

"Just Pembroke?"

She nodded. "That's all I ever heard."

I wrote the name down beneath the first.

Mara stared into her coffee now, the surface untouched. "After the disappearances started," she said, "I went to the Westbridges. Every time. I told them something was wrong."

"And?"

"They told me to do what Gareth said." Her jaw tightened. "And then they gave me raises. Big ones. Every time."

She looked up at me then, eyes clear and unflinching. "I didn't ask questions. I should have. But the money mattered. I was rebuilding my life after a terrible divorce. I told myself I was being paranoid."

I didn't interrupt her. I didn't offer absolution or judgment. I just listened.

"I don't have kids," she added quietly. "No one depending on me. I thought that made it easier. Safer."

"It didn't," I said. Not unkindly.

She nodded. "No."

I closed the notebook. "Would you be willing to sit with a police sketch artist to help us identify Mr. Pembroke? If I'm not able to track him down online."

Mara didn't hesitate. "Yes."

When we stood to leave, something had shifted—not just in what I knew, but in how I understood it.

The Ashford hadn't been corrupted.

It had been repurposed.

By the time I left the office that evening, the sky had already gone dark.

I walked to my car slower than usual, organizing the pieces as I went. Obsidian Venture Capital. Mr. Pembroke. Walker chasing the man with the key. Ray gone. Gareth dead.

Everything finally had a shape.

And that was what unsettled me most.

I finally knew where to look.

And I was well aware of the danger that came with it.

# CHAPTER 34

I ATE STANDING AT the counter.

Something I'd picked up on the way home—lukewarm by the time I unwrapped it, barely registering as food. I didn't bother sitting down. I didn't bother turning on more lights than I needed. The apartment felt neutral, familiar, the way it always did when I came back alone.

I set the container aside and opened my laptop.

Obsidian Venture Capital didn't hide. That was the first thing I noticed. No shell-company obfuscation, no deliberate opacity. Their website was polished, restrained, heavy on language about stewardship and long-term value.

They were big. Bigger than I'd expected.

Headquarters in London. Global offices. Infrastructure portfolios. Real estate holdings that crossed jurisdictions without friction. A firm that didn't buy companies to flip them, but to absorb them—quietly, permanently.

I scrolled.

Chairman of the Board: Alistair Pembroke.

British. Early seventies. Unmarried. A single formal

portrait—dark suit, neutral expression, eyes that gave nothing away. World traveler. Hands-on owner.

I leaned back slightly, letting that settle.

Hands-on didn't mean visible. It meant present. It meant proximity without fingerprints.

If Pembroke was involved, he wasn't moving the money himself. He had a whole network of operators below him. Men like Thomas Kline. Men like Ray Donnelly, who could profile the victims and access their apartments any time he wanted to. And other kinds of men. The kidnappers and killers, for example. Like the guys who tried to take me out. All of them had one thing in common. They could be replaced without consequence.

I closed the laptop and carried what was left of my dinner to the trash.

In the bathroom, I showered quickly, letting the heat work some of the stiffness out of my shoulders. I dressed the way I always did at night—T-shirt, underwear, nothing else—and moved through the apartment without thinking about it.

Routine had a way of convincing you things were under control.

I went to the bedroom and put my gun into the drawer on the nightstand. Picked up my Kindle and settled into bed, reading just long enough for my eyes to start drifting, the words blurring at the edges.

That was when I heard it.

Not a sound exactly. More like the absence of one. A click that didn't belong to the building settling or a neighbor moving around. Too precise. Too deliberate.

I set the Kindle down.

My hand went to the nightstand drawer without hesitation.

I stood slowly, the gun steady in my grip, and stepped into the hallway.

The apartment looked the same. Shadows where they belonged. Furniture undisturbed. But something had shifted. The air felt wrong—compressed, expectant.

I took another step.

That was as far as I got.

A blur of movement came from my left. A hard strike knocked the gun from my hand before I could fire. It skidded across the floor, disappearing under the couch.

I reacted on instinct.

I drove my elbow backward, felt it connect with something solid, heard a grunt. I turned into him, chopping down on his arm as he reached for me again. Something metallic hit the floor.

He swung with his other hand. The blow caught me on the side of the head, bright and disorienting, sending the room tilting.

I staggered but stayed upright.

I kicked him hard between the legs. He dropped to one knee, breath leaving him in a rush. I swung, felt my fist connect with his jaw, and he went down.

I lunged for the gun.

He was faster than I expected.

He tackled me from the side, driving us into the floor. The impact knocked the air out of my lungs. His weight came down hard, pinning me, both hands encircling my throat and squeezing.

I fought, bucked, tried to get leverage, but he was

stronger. He tightened his grip, and the edges of my vision began to darken.

I couldn't get him off.

The pressure increased. The world narrowed.

Then a gunshot tore through the room.

Blood and gore rained down on my face.

The hands around my throat released, and the man on top of me collapsed to the side.

I lay there gasping, air rushing back into my lungs in painful bursts, the ceiling spinning above me. Footsteps. A voice calling my name. It was Walker.

Walker dropped to his knees beside me, his face tight with focus, already checking me for injuries.

"You might have to go to the hospital," he said.

"I'm okay," I managed. "I think."

"I need to call this in," he said. "Uniforms will be on the way, and we need to be clear that the scene is under control."

He made the call. Took care of it. Then he stood and crossed the room. I heard fabric being pulled back, then his voice again—lower now.

"It was Reyes," he said. "He was the mole."

I rolled to my side and looked. Reyes's dead eyes looked back at me. The lower part of his jaw had been torn apart as the bullet passed out of his brain. Walker closed Reyes' eyes, then came back over to me. I was still on the floor.

"He'd gotten too nervous after the raid last night," he said. "Started during the ride. I was worried that since he knew where you lived, he might try something. So I followed him after he left the office tonight. When he stopped near your place, I knew."

He looked past me, toward the body on the floor.

"I think I would've been next," he said.

I nodded once, the reality of it settling in.

"Paperwork's going to be a nightmare," I said.

He didn't smile. "Worth it."

He reached for his phone.

"There's more," I said. "When you're ready."

"I'm ready," he said, "but you and I are going to be tied up for the next three or four hours, if not more."

He was right. There was a dead man on the floor of my apartment. And he was cop.

"Tomorrow morning?" I asked.

"Matt's?" he suggested. Matt's was a breakfast place that doubled as a cop hangout, just up Camelback a few blocks away.

I nodded.

"Around eight, then," he said.

There was a hard knock at the door. The uniforms had arrived. Walker and I would regroup tomorrow.

# CHAPTER 35

MATT'S BIG BREAKFAST sat just up Camelback, catty-corner from the Safeway—plain from the outside, stubbornly unglamorous, a place that didn't bother trying to be anything but what it was: breakfast, fast, loud, and honest.

I arrived a few minutes early and stood on the sidewalk for a second, letting the morning air work on me. It was the first day of February, and the sun was already up, already serious, throwing hard light across the parked cars and the low stucco strip behind the patio railing. When the sun came up in Phoenix, you felt it, even in wintertime.

Inside, the place was bright in that utilitarian way—concrete floor, long tables, white stools lined up like teeth. The open kitchen was all motion and metal. An orange wall behind the counter held shelves and bottles and the tools of people who knew what they were doing. On a white brick wall, a cartoon pig strolled across the paint, cheerful and dumb, like it had no idea what humans did to each other after midnight.

The smell hit first: coffee, bacon, butter, something sweet on the griddle. It should've been comforting.

It wasn't.

Comfort required sleep, and I felt like I'd been awake for a week. The police, detectives, medical officers and forensics had been in my apartment for hours. Both Walker and I were interviewed separately, and the boys in blue had finally understood that Reyes was a bad cop, that I was the victim, and that Walker was the good cop.

I found a small two-top near the edge of the room where I could see the door without looking obvious. Habit. Walker had rubbed off on me, or maybe I'd always been this way and just hadn't had a reason to admit it.

I stared at the menu without reading it. Words didn't want to behave yet.

A waitress came by with a coffee pot and a tired smile. "Coffee?"

"Yes," I said, because the alternative was lying down on the floor.

She poured, set down a mug, and moved on. I wrapped both hands around it like I could steal heat through my palms. The first sip was too hot, bitter, perfect.

Walker walked in a minute later—ball cap low, T-shirt under an open button-down, the kind of clothes cops wore when they wanted to look like they weren't cops. It never worked. His shoulders gave him away. His eyes gave him away. The fact that he scanned the room without moving his head gave him away.

He spotted me, and for a second, his face softened.

Then it tightened again.

He crossed the room and, on his way, nodded at a

couple of uniforms posted up at the counter with coffee. They nodded back. No smiles. Just recognition.

He slid into the seat across from me and exhaled like he'd been holding his breath since last night.

"You look like hell," he said.

"Likewise," I said.

He stared at me for a beat, then his gaze dropped—briefly—to where the bruise was forming along my jawline, and the stiff way I held my shoulders.

"How are you?" he asked, quieter now.

I could've lied. I didn't.

"I'm vertical," I said. "And I'm not dead."

He nodded once, as if filing it away. Then he glanced toward the waitress.

"Coffee," he said, when she approached. "Black."

She poured and left.

For a moment, we just sat there, two exhausted people in a room that smelled like pancakes, waiting for the adrenaline to stop pretending it was fuel.

It didn't stop.

It just thinned out, like a river dropping in summer, exposing rocks you hadn't seen when the current was high.

I tried to shake it off. "They have beer," I said, sliding the menu toward him like it was a dare.

He looked down at the menu, then back up at me. "At eight in the morning?"

"Just offering options," I said.

A corner of his mouth twitched. It wasn't quite a smile, but it was something.

He leaned forward slightly. "We didn't get to talk," he said.

"I know."

"Uniforms. Sergeants. Homicide. Everybody with a clipboard."

"Standard," I said.

"Not standard for me," he corrected. "He was my partner, and I killed him."

The words landed like an anvil.

Reyes. Jaw mostly gone. Dead eyes. Walker closing them like that was a kindness he didn't owe.

I stared into my coffee. "You saved my life."

His jaw clenched. "I did my job."

"Your job was compromised by a bad seed," I said.

He didn't argue.

Outside the window, traffic moved up Camelback like any other morning. People going to work. People shopping. People living lives untouched by what had happened on my floor.

"I found something last night," I said.

Walker's gaze sharpened. "About Reyes?"

I shook my head. "Not Reyes. About the whole thing."

He waited.

"Obsidian Venture Capital," I said.

His eyes narrowed a fraction.

"They acquired Westbridge two years ago," I said. "That's when the trouble started."

He stared past me, thinking.

"Two years," he said. "That tracks."

"And Ray Donnelly and Gareth Cole were hired shortly after," I said.

"You're sure?"

"I'm sure enough to say it out loud."

He took a sip of coffee.

"And Ray Donnelly?"

"Ray resigned yesterday."

Walker's face flashed. "Why didn't you tell me?"

"I just did."

"Why didn't you tell me sooner?"

"Because he was leaving town. He wasn't going to talk."

Walker leaned back, frustrated.

"What was I supposed to do?" I asked. "Hold him at gunpoint?"

A muscle jumped in his jaw.

"No," he said.

We sat in it.

The waitress came back. We ordered.

"What about the feds?" I asked.

"I passed it up the line."

"And?"

"No response yet."

"The system," I said.

"The system," he agreed.

"Facial recognition on the man with the key?" I asked.

"No results."

"None?"

"None."

"We need access to the FBI database," I said.

"That doesn't look like it's going to happen anytime soon," he said.

"Well, at least you're still employed."

He ignored my attempt at humor. "The trail went cold," he said.

I lowered my voice. "There's one more person who might help."

"Who?"

"Evan Pike," I said. "Apartment 109."

Walker paused. "Who's he?"

"A tenant at The Ashford. I think he knows something. A lot, maybe."

"What leads you to think that?" he asked.

"My gut."

He chuckled. No doubt he'd been in that same place a hundred times before. When every lead you've surfaced either didn't pan out or went cold. Or disappeared. When all you have left is your gut.

"The fight goes on then," he said.

"And the trail is running thin," I replied.

Our food arrived.

"You sure about this guy?" he asked.

"No," I said. "You mind doing a background check on him?"

He nodded. "Give me a day."

"No problem, but I'm going to talk to him today."

"Let's get together tomorrow to share our results."

"Copy that," I said, surprised by how much I'd missed the cadence of real police work.

"Watch your back," he said.

"I will. But if we don't keep moving, they win."

Walker nodded. "Then we keep moving."

# CHAPTER 36

I KNOCKED ON THE door to apartment 109 and waited.

It didn't take long for Evan Pike to answer it, and I was surprised to see him greet me with a smile as opposed to a scowl.

"I was wondering when I'd be hearing from you," he said. "Would you like to come in?"

His tone was casual. Almost warm. That, more than anything, made me hesitate.

The hallway was quiet—too quiet for midmorning—and the door stood open in a way that felt deliberate, like he wanted witnesses to know he wasn't hiding. I noted the distance back to the stairwell, the blind corner near the elevator, the fact that no one else was around to hear a raised voice. Whatever this was going to be, it was already past the point of discretion.

I stepped inside anyway.

Apartment 109 smelled faintly of coffee and ozone. The lights were low, the blinds half-drawn, the room crowded with equipment that didn't belong in a one-bedroom rental. Monitors lined the far wall, some dark, others alive with feeds I didn't immediately recognize. A folding table held a nest of cables, routers, hard drives stacked like bricks. The place felt temporary, improvised—functional rather than lived in.

I took in the layout automatically. One clear exit. Narrow kitchen. Nowhere to move fast without committing to it.

Evan closed the door behind me but didn't lock it.

"You're calmer than I expected," I said.

He shrugged. "You survived the night."

"I didn't know you were keeping score."

"I keep track of lots of things."

That twitchy energy I'd clocked before was still there, coiled under the surface, but now it felt focused. Directed. He gestured toward a chair at the small kitchen table. I didn't sit.

"You've been lurking around this building for months," I said. "Watching people. Watching me."

"Years," he corrected. "And yes."

No apology. No denial.

"Why?" I asked.

"Because something was wrong here," he said. "And because no one else was paying attention."

I folded my arms. "That's not an answer."

"It is if you know what you're looking at."

He crossed to the wall of monitors and tapped a key. One screen came alive, showing a grainy feed of the lobby—empty now, but unmistakable.

"You're running cameras," I said.

"Some of them."

"How many?"

"Enough."

I stepped closer, scanning the feeds. Stairwells. Service corridors. Places Ray had every right to be.

That was the trick. Ray didn't do the damage there. He used those spaces to disappear into the building—so no one noticed when he crossed into places he didn't belong.

Seeing it now, I understood how clean it had been.

"You know Ray was the spotter," I said.

Evan smiled faintly. "Of course I do."

I turned back to him. "How?"

"Because he was terrible at hiding it. He liked people. Liked talking. Liked knowing things about them. Who lived alone. Who had family. Who didn't."

My jaw tightened.

"And Gareth Cole?" I asked.

"Ran the numbers," Evan said. "Verified eligibility. Made sure the targets were AESS recipients. Gave verbal orders to seal the rooms of the missing people. Clean on paper. Quiet. Disposable."

"Ray went into their apartments," I said.

"When they were out," Evan agreed. "Pulled banking information. Account access. Everything the next phase needed."

"And the abductions?" I asked. "Where did they happen?"

"Not here," he said.

The answer landed heavier than I expected.

"They were flagged," he continued. "Tracked. Ray would alert the team when a target left the building. Schedule, routine, vulnerabilities. Then they vanished somewhere else. No return. No body. Just an absence.

And Gareth made sure no one on the outside ever found out about it. ”

“And the fraud,” I said.

“Started immediately,” he said. “The payments kept flowing. Then benefit redirection. Identity maintenance. A machine that only works if the disappearance isn’t logged by anyone.”

I stared at him. “How do you know all this?”

The monitors. The mixers. The recording equipment.

“I listen,” he said. “I watch. I log. I correlate.”

“You’re spying on the building,” I said.

“Yes.”

“Why?” I asked. “Are you working for a government agency?”

He snorted. “Nope.”

“Then what are you?”

He considered that. “I work in tech. Security architecture. Data aggregation. I guess I’m... nosy.”

“That’s not enough to explain this.”

“It is if you’re the kind of person who can’t unsee patterns.”

I felt the familiar anger rising. “Why didn’t you go to the police?”

Evan looked at me then, really looked at me.

“Why didn’t you?”

“I did,” I said. “Eventually.”

“And where did that get you?” he asked.

I thought of Reyes. Of my apartment floor. Of Walker standing over a dead man, already calculating what this would cost him.

I didn’t answer.

"Exactly," Evan said softly.

I exhaled, slow and controlled. "Then why are you telling me all this?"

"Because I know you're one of the good guys."

I started to laugh, but the sound caught when I remembered what Evan had said to me that night he'd been lurking outside the office while I'd been inside. *Be careful who you listen to in this place.*

At the time, I'd taken it as a warning. I hadn't realized he'd been offering help.

I looked at him again. "How do you know I'm one of the good guys?"

"You found most of my bugs in the penthouse," he said. "The cameras. The listening devices."

I felt my pulse jump. "Most?"

He smiled. "You didn't find all of them."

Cold slid down my spine.

"So it was you," I said. "You put all that stuff in there."

He nodded. "A few years back. And then the one I put in the picture frame, after you changed the lock."

"Why?"

"Because that's where the gravity was," he said. "And because it let me answer the question you haven't asked yet."

I held his gaze. "Who's running this operation?"

Evan's smile widened—not with pleasure, but with something like grim satisfaction.

"Pembroke," he said.

The name hung between us, heavy and inevitable.

I didn't speak.

I didn't have to.

# CHAPTER 37

"ALISTAIR PEMBROKE IS hands-on," Evan said. "Obsidian owns companies that are inherently well-suited for fraud. He has the system worked out, but it can't function without the right people at every level. That's why he personally interviews every candidate before they're hired. Every level. No exceptions."

He spoke evenly, like he was walking me through a blueprint.

"He interviewed Ray," Evan continued. "Then Gareth. Both of them. Right up there in the penthouse."

"And Mara?" I asked.

"No," he said. "She was already here, and he left it to the Westbridges to manage her."

"What about the Westbridges?" I asked. "How much did they know?"

"As little as possible," Evan said. "Whatever they knew came from Mara, and she didn't know much. Only that people were disappearing. Pembroke's operating order to them was simple: let Gareth Cole handle things at The Ashford. Don't ask questions."

"Or else," I said.

Evan nodded. "Exactly."

"Or else they'd disappear too."

"Yes."

I let that sit for a moment.

"Then why did the Westbridges hire me?" I asked, already knowing why, but wanting to see just how good Evan was at this.

"They wanted insulation," Evan said. "They wanted someone else to notice what they pretended not to see. Someone who might go to the police."

"So they could claim ignorance," I said. "Not just with law enforcement, but with Pembroke."

He inclined his head slightly. "They could say they hired you because they thought that was their responsibility. Maybe it would've been enough of an excuse. Maybe not."

"And now?" I asked.

"They're in serious trouble with Pembroke," Evan said. "Since you shut things down here, the system broke. That draws attention."

"Where does that leave me?" I asked.

"Same place I would be if they knew what I was doing," he said. "In the blast radius. Just like your buddy Walker."

I thought of Walker's words at Matt's Big Breakfast. *I think I would've been next.*

"You came to me because you already knew," he said finally. "You just needed confirmation."

"And you still opened the door," I said.

"Of course I did," he replied. "Because now we're on the same side."

I studied him—this man I'd written off as a threat, a shadow in stairwells and hallways—and felt something quietly reconfigure.

Evan Pike wasn't reckless. He wasn't playing spy. He wasn't chasing leverage or relevance. He was doing exactly what I was doing—what Walker was doing—but without a badge, without authority, without anyone watching his back.

He had seen something wrong and refused to look away.

The equipment in the apartment wasn't bravado. It wasn't obsession. It was infrastructure. A private attempt to impose order on something that had none. He'd built it carefully, methodically, knowing exactly what kind of attention it could attract if the wrong person ever noticed.

And he'd kept going anyway.

That was the part that shifted my assessment—not his competence, which I'd already clocked, but his commitment. He hadn't done this because it was safe or smart or likely to succeed. He'd done it because stopping would have meant accepting what was happening here.

He wasn't trapped the way people liked to imagine. He could leave—same as I could.

But leaving wouldn't erase what he knew.

For the first time since I'd taken the job at The Ashford, I didn't see him as a liability.

I saw him as someone who had chosen the same side I had—long before either of us knew what that choice would cost.

On the other hand, now that we were working together, he needed to understand some very basic ground rules.

"And Evan?" I said.

"Yes?"

"If you ever put another camera in my space without telling me—"

He lifted one hand. Not defensive. Not apologetic.

"You'll know."

It wasn't a promise.

It was a statement of fact.

I took an Uber to Duck and Decanter to meet Walker for lunch.

The place sat back from Camelback like it didn't want attention—low-slung, shaded by trees, the kind of spot you had to already know about to find. No big sign. No foot traffic spilling onto the sidewalk. Inside, it smelled like bread and coffee and something faintly herbal, the way old delis do when they've been doing the same thing well for decades.

Walker was already there, seated at a small table near the back, half-turned toward the room. Habit. He stood when he saw me, smiled, waited until I sat before dropping back into his chair.

"Nice call on this place," he said. "One of my favorites."

"Mine too," I said.

He nodded once. Approval, or at least agreement.

We ordered at the counter—sandwiches, iced tea for him, sparkling water for me—and didn't start talking until the plates were in front of us. Even then, Walker took a bite first, like he needed the normalcy of it.

"They assign you a new partner yet?" I asked.

"Not yet," he said. Then, after a beat, "Want the job?"

The line might've been a joke. Might not have been. Either way, it didn't land.

"I already told you," I said. "PPD won't hire me."

He nodded, unoffended. "Fair enough." Then, more serious: "What have you got?"

"You first," I said.

Walker wiped his hands on a napkin, folded it carefully, like he was buying himself time.

"Evan Pike checks out," he said. "No priors. No arrests. No financial weirdness. Works in IT. No degree, but steady employment. Keeps his nose clean. What did he tell you?"

"That Pembroke is the one running the whole thing."

Walker's eyebrows lifted. Just slightly. "Swinging for the fences, isn't he?"

"Maybe," I said. "But he's got some pretty solid intel."

Walker leaned back, scanned the room without making it obvious. "I don't see how we pin anything on a guy that high up the food chain. Especially since he's not even an American citizen and doesn't live here."

"Pembroke insists on meeting the people who work in his illicit operations," I said. "That's a strength, and a weakness—could be our opening."

"Could be," Walker said.

"Anything new on your end?" I asked.

"Yes," he said. "Since you ask."

He leaned forward now, forearms on the table.

"We're getting hits on most of the guys you photographed. All except the head guy. He's a ghost."

"Maintenance?" I asked.

"Mostly," Walker said. "Buildings like The Ashford. Same access points. Same routines. Almost all of them have priors, which is how we could ID them."

"Makes sense," I said.

"So it looks like we're going to be able to shut this operation down in Phoenix," he said. "All because of you."

I stared at my sandwich. The bread had gone soft where the dressing soaked in.

"Then how come I don't feel like it's over?" I asked.

Walker didn't answer right away.

"Probably because we both know it'll just pop up somewhere else," he said finally. "Different buildings. Different city. Same system."

"Because we didn't shut down the mastermind," I said.

"No," he agreed. "We didn't."

I took a sip of water. The room felt quieter than it should have.

"Did you ever interview the Westbridges?" I asked.

"Yesterday afternoon," Walker said.

"And?"

"They kept their hands clean," he said. "Even while everything underneath them was on fire."

"I figured," I said.

That's when my phone buzzed.

I glanced down, then froze for half a second too long before I caught myself.

Elaine Westbridge.

*Can you come by our office right away?*

"Speak of the devil," I said.

Walker looked at me. “The Westbridges?”

I nodded.

He exhaled through his nose. “Hope it’s not bad news for you.”

“Why would it be?” I asked.

“Well,” he said, “you cleaned up their mess. Hard to see why they’d want to keep you around. Not that you can’t do the job—but it’s not really your thing, is it?”

“I haven’t been there long enough to find out,” I said.

He gave me a look then. Something unreadable. Something like he was filing the moment away.

“Well, good luck,” he said.

“You too,” I replied.

We stood. He hesitated, like he might say something else, then thought better of it. Another habit.

I watched him walk out first, blending into the early afternoon like he’d done it a thousand times before.

And that was the last time I ever saw Jim Walker.

# CHAPTER 38

THE CONFERENCE ROOM at Westbridge Property Management was already occupied when I arrived.

Elaine Westbridge sat at the far end of the table, posture perfect, hands folded as if she'd practiced the position. Mark Westbridge was beside her, jacket off, sleeves rolled, eyes tired in the way of men who believed competence could insulate them from consequences.

And at the head of the table sat a man I hadn't met—but recognized anyway.

Alistair Pembroke.

The air in the room shifted the moment I registered him. Not because he moved. He didn't. Not because he looked dangerous. He didn't. It was the opposite. He looked composed in a way that suggested nothing here could surprise him.

He was in his seventies, silver hair combed neatly back from a high forehead, the lines in his face the kind earned by long habit rather than hardship. His suit was dark charcoal, perfectly cut, the kind that didn't advertise expense because it didn't need to. White shirt.

Conservative tie. Everything restrained. Everything deliberate.

British, unmistakably so. Not in accent alone, but in bearing. In the way he occupied the space as if it belonged to him by precedent.

I felt my shoulders tighten.

I stepped into the room, closed the door behind me, and took the empty chair at the far end of the table, facing him from a distance. As I sat, I pulled my blazer back just enough to reveal the grip of the gun at my hip. Not a threat. Not a warning. A fact.

Pembroke's eyes flicked there—quick, acknowledging—then returned to my face.

No reaction. No comment.

*Good*, I thought. Or very bad.

"Kate," Elaine said, standing. "Thank you for coming so quickly."

She gestured toward the man at the head of the table. "This is Alistair Pembroke. He owns Westbridge."

Pembroke stood, walked the length of the table to my end, and offered his hand. I rose and shook it.

His grip was firm but brief. His palm warm. His smile polite.

"Ms. Mercer," he said. "It's a pleasure."

The accent was clipped, educated, and formal. I gave nothing back.

"Likewise," I said.

Pembroke returned to his end of the table.

We sat.

The Westbridges said nothing further. That was telling.

Pembroke folded his hands on the table, as if concluding a meeting that had already been underway.

"I wanted to personally thank you for cleaning up the mess at The Ashford," he said.

The words were precise. No apology. No admission. Mess, as if it were an operational inconvenience.

"You may not know this," he continued, "but when I acquired Westbridge, I also acquired the majority of the buildings under its management, including The Ashford. Westbridge alone would have been too small to justify the effort. But it was... a natural gateway to the kind of real estate Obsidian finds attractive."

I held my tongue.

Evan's words surfaced uninvited. *Companies already primed for certain systems.*

Pembroke went on. "I personally approved your hiring. You've performed admirably. I was appalled to hear of the attacks on your person, and I'm grateful you survived."

His gaze flicked—just briefly—to my gun.

"Now," he said, "we must ensure you are removed from harm's way."

*This should be interesting*, I thought.

"And how do you propose to do that?" I asked.

"Your work here is done," Pembroke said smoothly. "We'd like to transfer you to another Obsidian property in Europe. One experiencing a similar... difficulties. Your skill set would be most useful in correcting it."

I tilted my head. "What property?"

"A high-profile hotel," he said. "The Valmont Palace."

"And the problem?" I asked.

"Missing guests," he said.

I didn't blink.

"And why don't you go to the police?" I asked.

"For the same reason we didn't in this case," Pembroke replied. "Bad publicity."

I leaned back slightly. "Well, thank you for thinking of me. But I'm happy working at The Ashford."

Pembroke's eyebrows lifted. A fraction.

"Oh," he said. "I see I've gotten ahead of myself. Elaine? Mark?"

Elaine cleared her throat.

"Kate," she said carefully, "you've been wonderful. Truly. But as it turns out, your skills aren't entirely compatible with the needs of a smoothly functioning building."

There it was.

"We're going to have to let you go. With a generous severance, of course."

The room went very quiet.

"Okay," I said, standing.

Pembroke raised a hand.

"Ms. Mercer," he said. "If you and I could speak privately, I think it would be helpful."

"To whom?" I asked.

He smiled then. Not warmly. Not coldly. With interest.

"To both of us," he said. "Please."

I sat.

Elaine and Mark rose without protest and left the room.

Pembroke waited until the door closed.

"It may be useful if we clear the air," he said. "Am I

right in assuming you suspect me of involvement in the illicit activities at The Ashford?"

I didn't answer.

Instead, I asked, "Why did you interview Ray Donnelly and Gareth Cole?"

If the question surprised him, he didn't show it.

"I was in Phoenix conducting annual site visits," he said. "The Westbridges were hiring. Staff upgrades are a requirement when Obsidian takes over a property. They were kind enough to put me up in the penthouse, which made the meetings convenient."

"And yet you hired them," I said. "Two crooks."

"I assure you their background checks were clean," Pembroke replied. "Otherwise, they wouldn't have been hired."

I made a mental note to confirm that with Walker.

"We're prepared to triple your salary," Pembroke continued. "And provide accommodations at the Valmont Palace that far exceed anything at The Ashford."

That was a lot of money.

And his explanation—damn it—was plausible.

More than that, if Pembroke was the man behind it all, this was my best chance to get close enough to see how the machine really worked.

"I'd need to bring staff with me," I said.

"Oh?" Pembroke said. "Who?"

"Mara Feldman," I said. "She'd need placement in the hotel's administrative office."

"That makes sense," he said. "Approved."

"And Evan Pike," I added. "My IT man."

Pembroke frowned slightly. "I don't know him."

*Good*, I thought. Evan had stayed invisible.

"So he's approved?" I asked.

"Of course," Pembroke said. "Anyone else?"

"That would be it. Except, I have one more question."

"Please," he said.

"Assuming my team and I get to the bottom of the problem in Amsterdam, what happens to us then? Will we still be employed?"

Pembroke didn't hesitate.

"Kate, Obsidian does not build temporary structures. If you solve Amsterdam, we'll find you something worthy of your team's attention."

He held my gaze for a moment longer, as if weighing how much to reveal.

"There are...other properties. Other irregularities. I prefer to place capable people where discretion is required."

"Sounds exciting," I said.

"From my view, you and your team are an investment. Long term."

"Thank you."

Pembroke stood. "Very well. I look forward to working with you, Katherine. May I call you Katherine?"

"Kate."

"Very well," he said, and approached me. "Here is my card, which includes my executive assistant, Miranda Baines's contact information. Please email or text her if you have further questions. I've left all the paperwork needed to get you started in your new position with Elaine and Mark. I'm sorry to depart so quickly, but I've got a plane to catch."

With that, Allistair Pembroke shook my hand and departed.

I left Westbridge Property Management with a signed severance agreement in my bag, a big severance check, and an offer that stretched halfway across the world.

Outside, the sun was bright. The sky was clear. Phoenix at its most honest.

I stood there for a moment, feeling the weight of what I'd agreed to without quite agreeing. Of what I'd lost. Of what I'd stepped toward.

I thought of Walker. Of Evan. Of the building I'd cleaned without truly purging.

I felt excitement.

And dread.

And something else, too.

Validation.

A week later, it got complicated.

# CHAPTER 39

*One Week Later*

THE DAY I left Phoenix, the sky looked scrubbed clean—winter-blue, too bright, the kind of day that made the city feel newly washed and harmless.

It was almost funny, how quickly life could do that. How quickly it could pretend.

My apartment was stripped down and empty. The lease ended at the end of the month, so I was leaving a bit early. Didn't matter.

Suitcase by the door. Passport on the counter. Phone fully charged. A folder of paperwork in my tote—severance, transfer documents, and the kind of corporate forms that made everything feel official, even when your instincts were screaming that nothing about it was normal.

I'd stood in the kitchen and stared at the counter for a full minute before I left, letting myself absorb it.

A week ago, I'd walked out of Westbridge Property Management, fired. And hired.

Today, I was headed to Europe on an executive transfer, with more money in my account than I'd had in a long time.

It felt like an awards ceremony no one had invited the public to.

The severance had hit my bank the next morning—generous, clean, immediate. Elaine's voice in my head: *We want to do right by you, Kate.* Pembroke's hand, warm and brief, his smile polite. The whole thing wrapped in courtesy.

As if courtesy could launder anything.

I'd spent the last seven days building a team.

Mara took the offer in stunned silence. She didn't even speak at first—just stared at me across the office desk at The Ashford, blinking like I'd told her the building was going to lift off its foundation and float away. When I told her the salary number, she let out a breath that sounded like a laugh and a sob at the same time.

"You're serious," she whispered.

"I'm serious," I said.

It took her two days to say yes. Two days to wrap her life around the idea that she'd be working in another place where guests disappeared and no one called the police because it was inconvenient. But when she came back to me, she was enthusiastic. Resolved.

"I'll give my two weeks' notice today," she said.

Evan's yes had been faster, after we cleared one hurdle. He had believed Pembroke to be the mastermind behind the criminal operation that had afflicted The Ashford. I told him what Pembroke had said about the interviews he conducted with Ray and Gareth Cole in the penthouse. He thought about it, then said, "Okay. I suppose we'll have the chance to figure out if he's telling the truth after we get to Amsterdam."

"That's what I thought," I said. "I take it you're in, then."

He nodded. "I'm in."

Not eager. Not giddy.

Just... inevitable.

"I'll need time," he'd said, eyes already moving as if he were calculating logistics. "Two weeks. Minimum. I have leases. Contracts. Hardware."

"Pembroke approved you," I told him. "You can come when you come."

That made Evan smile, but it didn't reach his eyes.

"Of course he did," he said. "He doesn't know me."

Thus, we'd agreed that Mara and Evan would follow me to Europe two weeks after I departed. Time to settle affairs stateside. Time to pack, to finish up with their jobs, to disappear cleanly from a life that still had roots in Phoenix.

I told myself I liked that.

I told myself it meant control.

I told myself a lot of things.

The one thing I didn't like was the gun.

Or rather—what I didn't like was leaving without it.

I'd spent enough time armed in the past month that unarmed now felt like stepping outside without shoes. But Europe wasn't Arizona. The problem wasn't how to get a weapon to the airport. The problem was what happened on the other side of the ocean.

I wasn't naive. I knew what strict meant when it came

to firearms in places like the Netherlands. I knew I wasn't going to land in a foreign country, walk into a shop, and buy peace of mind.

So I'd made a plan—half-formed, not yet actionable. Something I could tell myself as I zipped the suitcase and locked the door.

Temporary, I thought.

I'll fix it when I land.

The Uber Black pulled up right on time.

Glossy sedan. Clean interior.

The driver stepped out without a word and placed my bag in the trunk, movements economical, practiced.

By the time I slid into the back seat, he was already behind the wheel again—collared shirt, one hand resting on it, the other near the console, as if he'd been carved into that position.

The air smelled faintly of cologne and the synthetic lemon of a recently wiped dashboard.

"Sky Harbor, right?" the driver asked.

His accent was Russian. Or something close to it. Hard consonants, rounded vowels. It didn't alarm me on its own—Phoenix had taught me that accents were as common as dust—but it registered anyway. Everything registered now.

"Yes," I said. "Terminal 4."

He glanced at the rearview mirror. His eyes met mine for a fraction too long, then returned to the road.

"Terminal 4," he repeated.

We pulled away from the curb.

The city slid past in neat blocks. Coffee shops opening their doors. People in gym clothes and sunglasses.

A woman walking a dog that looked like it belonged to someone who never worried about money.

I should have felt relief.

I did, in a way.

The Ashford was behind me. Reyes was dead. Ray was gone. Kline was gone. The maintenance men were being identified. The Westbridges had shoved me off their ledger with a polite smile and a severance check that told me more than their words ever had.

And Pembroke—

I thought of him the way you think of a storm you can see far out over the desert. Not here yet. But coming.

Still, there was a part of me that couldn't help it.

A small, stubborn satisfaction.

I'd walked into that building and found rot. I'd ripped it open. I'd lived.

Now I was being paid for it.

The 51 carried us south. The skyline in the distance looked sharp against the sky, glass and steel and certainty.

I checked my phone again—no new messages. Mara had sent a simple text at six that morning: *Safe travels. Let me know you landed.* Evan had sent nothing at all, which was its own kind of communication.

The driver didn't speak.

His silence should have been neutral.

Instead it felt… curated.

I watched the back of his head. The way his shoulders stayed square. The way he didn't fidget. The way his driving was smooth without being casual, like he knew the exact speed that looked normal.

I told myself I was being paranoid.

I told myself paranoia was what had kept me alive.

We approached an exit, and I sat up slightly as I saw the sign.

Not the airport.

McDowell Road.

My stomach tightened.

The car drifted right.

"Hey," I said sharply. "What are you doing?"

No response.

The sedan moved off the freeway with the same smooth confidence it had held the entire ride.

"Wrong exit," I said, louder. "You missed the airport."

His eyes flicked to the mirror again.

This time, he didn't look away quickly.

"Traffic," he said. "Shortcut."

"That's not a shortcut," I said.

The street opened up ahead—wide lanes, low buildings, a stretch of industrial frontage that looked empty even in daylight. The kind of landscape that didn't belong to anyone, which meant it could belong to anyone.

"Pull over," I said.

The driver's hand moved—casual, almost lazy—toward a control on the door panel.

A faint mechanical hum answered him.

Something slid up between the front and back seats.

A clear partition.

For half a second, my mind refused to accept it. It didn't belong in a rideshare car. Not like that. Not rising cleanly, smoothly, locking into place as if it had been built for this exact moment.

"Stop the car," I yelled, voice sharp enough to cut through my own disbelief.

The driver didn't turn around.

He didn't have to.

The air changed.

At first, it was subtle—an odd sweetness, like a cleaning solvent warmed by sunlight. Then it thickened, heavy in my throat, creeping up into my sinuses.

I knew what it was when I saw the driver slip on a respirator.

I coughed once.

Then again.

My eyes started to water.

"No," I said, and the word came out broken, already fraying at the edges.

I reached for the window switch and pressed down hard.

Nothing.

Pressed again.

Nothing.

I leaned forward and hammered the glass with the side of my fist.

The partition didn't even shiver.

Panic tried to rise. I shoved it down, forcing my brain to work.

Door.

I grabbed the handle and yanked.

Locked.

I yanked again, harder, as if force could rewrite engineering.

The door didn't move.

Child lock.

Of course it was a child lock.

I pulled the handle until my knuckles ached, then slammed my shoulder into the door, trying to jar it, to make it give, to make it do anything but hold.

The car stayed steady, gliding forward.

The driver's silhouette didn't change.

He didn't hurry. He didn't flinch. He drove like he was taking me to a business meeting.

My lungs burned.

I dragged in another breath and it tasted like syrup and metal.

I fumbled for my phone, hands clumsy now, the screen too bright, the icons too far away. I tried to call 911.

My thumb missed.

I tried again.

My vision swam.

The cough that came out of me wasn't loud anymore. It was wet. Ineffective. Like my body already knew it was losing.

The world narrowed to sensation: the sting in my eyes, the pressure in my skull, the absurd calm of the driver's shoulders.

I thought of Mara.

I thought of Evan.

I thought of Pembroke's polite smile and the way the Westbridges hadn't met my eyes when they fired me.

And then, as the darkness pressed in from the edges, one clear thought cut through everything—sharp, simple, undeniable:

*I didn't know who had done this.*
The car kept moving.
And everything went black.

To be continued in Book 2 of *The Kate Mercer Files*:

*The Man With The Key.*

Purchase *The Man With The Key:*

Read on for a preview of *The Man With The Key.*

## THE MAN WITH THE KEY

D.L. MADDOX

Book 2 in The Kate Mercer Files

**Kate Mercer survived the conspiracy that tried to bury her.**

**Now she's following it to Amsterdam.**

Nine wealthy guests vanish from one of Europe's most exclusive hotels.

Their money disappears with them.

Kate is hired to take control of the Valmont Palace in Amsterdam—and to quietly uncover what happened to the missing guests no one is publicly searching for.

The hotel's management insists there's no scandal. No crime. Just wealthy travelers who left without checking out.

But the abandoned luggage tells a different story.

So do the private accounts being methodically drained.

As Kate digs into hotel records, staff loyalties, and the wealth management firms tied to the property, she recognizes the architecture.

**The same patterns that destroyed her career in Phoenix.**

**The same network that had infiltrated The Ashford.**

This isn't a new case.

It's the next layer of the conspiracy she refused to stop investigating.

And this time, she's not walking away.

Somewhere inside the labyrinth is a man who holds the key—to a secret meeting, to a financial network designed to erase people without consequence, and possibly to the trap closing around her.

The deeper Kate goes, the clearer it becomes:

She wasn't hired to investigate.

**She was sent into something that refuses to be found.**

**And destroys anyone who tries.**

Book 2 in The Kate Mercer Files.

# LETTER FROM D.L. MADDOX

Thank you so much for reading *The Super*. If you enjoyed it, I could really use your help. Some people don't realize that reviews and ratings are the lifeblood of any book. They can make all the difference in bringing books to a greater audience.

If you'd like to give me a helping hand, please take a minute or two to post a review for *The Super* on Amazon.

The link or QR code below will take you *directly* to the Review Page for *The Super*.

Thank you for reading my book! I hope you enjoy the other books in the series as well.

Sincerely,
D.L. Maddox

# ABOUT THE AUTHOR

D.L. Maddox is the pen name of an established fiction writer whose work explores human behavior, identity, and survival. The use of a pen name reflects a creative choice—designed to align with the unique voice, themes, and characters of these books—rather than a concealment of identity.

Maddox's thrillers are driven by emotional realism, layered suspense, and protagonists who confront danger with resilience and complexity. While the stories are fictional, the psychological forces at play are grounded in deep research and experience.

www.ingramcontent.com/pod-product-compliance
Lightning Source LLC
LaVergne TN
LVHW010643110826
845149LV00014B/2932
* 9 7 9 8 9 9 3 2 6 7 5 4 8 *